TOM MALONE

Ghosts of Machu Picchu

Library of Congress Control Number: 2022900102

First edition

ISBN: 978-1-945236-20-4

This book was professionally typeset on Reedsy. Find out more at reedsy.com

To those who paved the way.

"I will live in the past, the present, and the future. The spirits of all three shall strive within me. I will not shut out the lessons that they teach."

- Charles Dickens, A Christmas Carol

Prologue

D eep in the Andes Mountains of Peru lies a magical city. A city of wonder, of ancient history that remains engulfed by the jungle. A city that looms in the most mysterious segments of our imaginations.

Machu Picchu sits atop a jagged, vertical peak. Surrounded by the outer reaches of the Amazon River Basin, the area is shrouded by dense jungle. The Urubamba River runs underneath the city, echoing off of canyon walls, drowning out any noise from the city above it. Fog clings to the mountain tops, hiding the city from those who seek it.

Without the use of the wheel or large beasts of burden, Inca architects constructed the hidden city sometime around 1450, just as the Inca civilization reached its golden era. Built without mortar, builders had to carve stone with precision. Each stone fit together like a puzzle piece with connections so tight that a piece of paper could not fit between any crease. Situated along the Ring of Fire, the Andes Mountains brought frequent earthquakes, but Machu Picchu's flexible design allowed it to bend and sway while maintaining its strength and integrity.

Even with the advances of modern technology, historians have had difficulty deciphering the way that ancient architects built the city.

While the construction method of Machu Picchu remains a mystery, so does its purpose. This mystery has generated debate among Western historians. Some think that Machu Picchu was a vacation home for the ruler of the Inca. Others claim it was a religious site. A few historians have argued that Machu Picchu was simply a small city, an outpost of the Inca Empire.

And perhaps they're all right in some way.

Machu Picchu was placed in precise astrological alignment with constellations that played key roles in the Inca religion. And Inca religion played a prominent role in daily life. The ruler of the Inca people was the major figure in Inca religion, tying everything together.

But the purpose of Machu Picchu, and how it was built, remains a mystery.

* * *

The city of Cusco served as the Inca's center of power and culture. Structured in the shape of a puma, Cusco is nestled between mountains that surround it in all directions. Sitting at 12,000 feet of elevation, this expertly designed ancient city was home to massive religious temples, homes, farms, and royal seats of power, from which the ruler of the Inca people could command his territory.

Royal runners would carry messages from Cusco to the outlying cities of the empire. Running dozens of miles on foot through rugged terrain and extreme elevation levels, these runners were the links that kept the empire moving efficiently.

Until Spanish invaders arrived in 1532.

With guns, diseases, and greed, Spanish *conquistadors* destroyed Cusco, leveling it almost completely. The Spanish built

Catholic churches on top of toppled Inca temples, using the stones from the same temples they had destroyed. They built *haciendas* over the ruins of former Inca homes. They persecuted people who spoke Quechua. They attempted to eliminate all recollections of Inca traditions. All in the pursuit of gold and silver.

Spanish invaders pushed deeper into the Andes Mountains, but the Inca royal runners moved faster. The runners reached Machu Picchu and relayed the destruction of Cusco and the treachery of the Spanish.

According to legend, the inhabitants of Machu Picchu buried the city in vegetation. They blocked the only entrance to the city with boulders. And then, they vanished.

As Spanish *conquistadors* searched for hidden Inca treasures along the Urubamba River, they passed beneath Machu Picchu, completely unaware that a cultural treasure rose above them, clouded in mist.

Back in Cusco, the Spanish captured Tupac Amaru, the last Inca ruler to fight against Spanish invasion. The Spanish decapitated him and placed his head on a spike in the center of the city: Plaza de Armas.

* * *

In 1911, Hiram Bingham wandered through the Andes Mountains on an assignment from Yale University to find the lost city of the Inca. After speaking with a few Andean farmers (who still spoke Quechua), Bingham was brought to a city that stood atop a mountain above the Urubamba River. Aside from a few terraces that had been used by local farmers for generations, the stone city was covered in jungle.

Machu Picchu, untouched by the Spanish, had been preserved by Andean farmers since the days of Spanish invasion.

Bingham brought his newfound awareness of Machu Picchu to Western popular culture. As the years progressed, the ancient city in the sky became a pilgrimage destination for those seeking adventure, clarity, and fulfillment.

Machu Picchu possesses a certain mystique, an aura of mythology that has gripped adventurers for centuries. The mists that hang around Machu Picchu are said to contain spirits, the souls of ancestors who have come before us. Local legends contain stories of ghosts, spirits trapped within Machu Picchu's sphere of influence. Sometimes, these stories contain spirits who use their persuasion to keep unworthy people from entering into the sacred city. In other stories, ghosts follow travelers, testing their will, forcing them to prove their worthiness to visit the ruins. These legends have only added to the mysteries of Machu Picchu.

What follows is one such story.

Chapter 1

Sunlight snuck around skyscrapers and shined into Quinn's office through half-open blinds. The glare on his computer screen became unbearable, so he stood and walked to the window. A minor inconvenience, but he needed to step away from his screen anyway. Quinn had arrived at the office before sunrise again, this time to finalize the presentation slides that he would use during his proposal to the executive board.

He had been working on the project for two weeks. Late nights at the office, followed by early mornings. The data collection process overwhelmed him at times, especially when the data proved insufficient. Or worse, when it didn't help his cause. And the digital design of the presentation itself proved difficult, as the company had recently migrated to a new, unfamiliar software package.

Luckily, his building featured a coffee stand on his floor. After his fourth cup of the morning, he finally manufactured enough energy to complete the final slide.

Sipping his coffee, he looked out the window that overlooked the city. Far below, taxis hurried business people from one meeting to another. Ships pushed cargo from port to port. Kids sprinted from subways and buses on their way to school.

Cranes moved beams around the city, which seemed to expand perpetually, growing larger each day. This was the city coming to life.

Unaware of the wall clock, Quinn pulled his phone from his pocket and checked the time. He still had ten minutes until his meeting started. Turning away from the window, he walked slowly back toward his desk. It was a sleek desk, the kind he had always dreamed of having. It had a small globe. A fountain pen set that looked impressive, even though he didn't know how to use it. A tall leather chair. The inlaid bookshelf behind his desk featured a few crystal awards he had earned as a young associate at the company, a collection of his life's accomplishments.

Something caught his attention, snapping him from his self-admiration. Two members of the executive board walked by Quinn's office window toward the boardroom. They didn't see Quinn in his office, but he certainly noticed their presence.

They're early, he thought.

Quinn chugged the last few ounces of his coffee and tossed the paper cup in the trash bin. The cup sunk. Quinn clenching his fist, reminiscent of juvenile accomplishment. He straightened his tie, grabbed his leather portfolio, and walked into the hallway. As he strolled toward the boardroom, he attempted to project confidence.

Quinn's heart pounded as he approached the boardroom door. He took a deep breath and opened it, strutting in with the swagger he had seen other board members project in countless presentations.

"Good morning, gentlemen," Quinn said.

A man in an expensive suit nodded from a seat at the center of the table.

"Good morning, Mr. Thomas," the man said.

Quinn walked to the front of the room and set his leather portfolio on the podium. Turning on the board, he pulled up his presentation. The silent boardroom heightened his nerves. He felt judgmental stares from the ten executives who sat around the table. They all looked the same: white, middle-aged men from the upper socioeconomic class. All probably from the same part of the country, maybe even the same type of liberal arts college. A lot like himself. Only they were much older.

He opened his portfolio to occupy some time before he needed to speak; the portfolio was empty, just a prop, but he thought it made him look important and composed.

Beneath his calm facade, adrenaline coursed through his veins. Anxiety gripped his lungs. But he knew that he couldn't show it; these guys could smell fear, and fear was weakness. Taking a final deep breath, he spoke.

"Gentlemen," Quinn said, "thank you for taking the time to be here today. I'm Quinn Thomas, and I have a plan to make our company a lot more money."

* * *

When Quinn walked in, Lucy was dancing with her friends in the middle of the rooftop bar. She wore another new dress, this time from a boutique uptown. Spotting Quinn, Lucy waved frantically for him to join the dancing. He weaved through the crowd, dodging elbows and drinks before he reached the group.

"Hey, baby!" Lucy shouted over the music. "How'd the big pitch go?"

Quinn smiled proudly.

"I nailed it," he said.

"Of course you did!" Lucy shouted, her voice amplified by too many drinks.

She looked at her friends and pointed to Quinn.

"My man is about to be a big shot in this city," she shouted. "Drinks all around, ladies!"

Lucy's friends cheered. Quinn ducked his head and rubbed his neck. His eyes hurt from looking at a screen for such an extensive amount of time. And his temples throbbed from embarrassment.

"I'm going to go get myself a drink," Quinn said. "Can I get you something?"

"A shot of their best tequila," Lucy said. "Thanks, Quinny Bear."

Quinn suppressed the urge to gag. He didn't know what had upset him more: the drink order or the nickname that Lucy had started calling him.

Lucy was gorgeous, though. And she needed him. Or, she acted like she needed him. Sometimes, Quinn enjoyed it. Lucy's neediness made him feel a sense of power, a sense of importance.

He wanted to propose to her soon and solidify the connection between his family and hers. Not so much the connection to his own family. Quinn wanted to be connected to hers. Lucy's parents were influential in the city's business and philanthropic circles. And they would be instrumental in helping Quinn rise in the city's high societal ranks.

Quinn looked at Lucy. She danced with her friends. She danced as if she didn't have a care in the world. And, as far as Quinn could figure, she didn't. She seemed completely content with her upper class existence, content with living a life of mediocrity, content with having it all.

A sense of annoyance crept into Quinn's nerves. The concept

of contentment, of being fine with just living, seemed to take the fun out of life. The drive, the desire to acquire more. That was living.

Quinn elbowed his way up to the bar and ordered a beer and a mid-shelf tequila for Lucy. He knew that part of his own irritation came from his own stress at work. And lack of sleep.

As he approached Lucy's group again, he handed her the tequila glass. She looked at it quizzically.

"I thought you were getting tequila for all my friends," Lucy said.

Her obliviousness jabbed at Quinn's annoyance. He blinked his green eyes and held them closed a little longer than necessary. He sipped his beer quickly.

"Hey, I'm not feeling too well," Quinn said. "It was a long week."

"Just have another drink and it'll make you feel better," Lucy said, laughing to her friends.

"Not tonight," Quinn said. "I'm actually going to head out and go to bed."

Lucy turned her lip into a pout and clung to Quinn's arm.

"Stay out with us, Quinny Bear," she said.

"I really just need to go to bed," Quinn said. "But I'll call you tomorrow. Have fun with your friends."

He waved to Lucy's friends, and then kissed Lucy on the cheek. As he moved through the crowd, he set his pint glass on an empty table. He pushed the double doors open and strolled into the hallway. The line for the elevator was long, so he took the stairs.

The bass vibrated from the bar and echoed through the staircase. Eventually, the noise faded and Quinn found himself alone with nothing but his thoughts. It made him uncomfortable. He sped up his descent until he emerged onto the street. A wave of brisk night air contrasted the artificial heat from within the building.

The city was alive, buzzing with neon lights, sirens, and chatter. But, as he continued his walk, he noticed people looking at their phones, absorbed in their own realities. Eye contact with a kind stranger seemed unlikely.

As he walked, he replayed his meeting in the boardroom. The executives received his message well and agreed to enact his proposal. On paper, the meeting was a success. But something was missing. Somehow, even when he should have felt pride from his accomplishment, Quinn still felt a void.

Eventually, he reached his apartment entrance. As he reached for his keys, he paused and looked up at the clear night sky. He couldn't see any stars; too much light pollution from the city.

Putting his key into the lock, he began to climb up the stairs to his apartment, empty.

Chapter 2

The city hadn't fully woken up yet. Quinn moved along the smooth sidewalk toward his office building. His office's skyscraper didn't stand out prominently among the other towers that surrounded it; rather, it blended in. Just another tall building among the steel skyline.

Sewers wafted city scents of pungent steam. Construction zones, already churning in the early morning, lifted the aroma of tar and asphalt on the light breeze. City grates sent the clanking of metal echoing into the depths of the city, hidden below the tons of steel and cement that supported the city's ecosystem of coffee, cigarettes, and footsteps.

Stepping into the revolving door, Quinn emerged and walked through the elegant, sterile plaza. The cavernous space was nearly empty. A false chandelier hung from the ceiling above the stairs that led to a series of elevators.

"Happy Friday," a custodian shouted.

Lost in thought and habit, Quinn ignored the friendly gesture. Slapping the elevator button, Quinn waited, tapping his hand against his watch. Finally, the elevator door opened, revealing an empty cabin. Quinn stood in the cabin alone, relieved that he didn't have to feign interest and pleasantries with someone who he would likely never see again.

The ride to his floor seemed to drag on, a byproduct of working on an upper floor. In fact, his entire week had seemed to pass slowly.

The elevator door was gilded with gold. Quinn caught his own reflection, distorted by the warped metal. He noticed a glow behind him, lights that seemed to shimmer and disappear with the elevator's movement. Suddenly, Quinn felt a presence beside him. Looking over his shoulder, he found himself still alone on the elevator. He dismissed the feeling altogether.

But the sentiment still left him feeling unnerved. The elevator speed seemed to slow. Quinn needed to get out of the cabin.

Finally, the doors opened and Quinn bolted from the cabin.

Running on little sleep as usual, Quinn decided to stop at the coffee stand on his floor, where he ordered an espresso. He chugged it and tossed the paper cup into the trash, a motion that was becoming routine.

He passed by countless cubicles, some that belonged to employees from his division and some that belonged to other segments of the company. He hadn't met many people that worked in this section of the office, the section that the executive board referred to as "the Pit."

Quinn pushed open the door to his office. The shades were open, but the room remained dark; the sun hadn't come close to rising above the water, much less the surrounding skyscrapers. Tossing his briefcase onto his meticulously organized desk, he sunk into his chair.

He knew the money was coming. The executive board had agreed to his proposal. He assumed that a title increase would follow. Probably something ambiguous, like Director of Operations, or Senior Advisor. Advisor to what, nobody would be able to pin down.

Quinn dug his face into his palms and ran his fingers through his immaculately prepared hair. The late nights and early mornings were catching up to him. And the weekends at the office, or out for drinks with clients. The burden of work sat heavily on his shoulders.

And it was only going to increase.

But this is what he had always wanted. A major title at a prominent firm. A big salary. A lavish, city-driven lifestyle. And a beautiful girl by his side, his trophy for conquering the world.

I can't turn that down, Quinn thought.

As the sun rose, light caught dust and window blemishes, sending beams into his office. Quinn churned through statistics and graphs, responding to emails with fury. He wanted to put work behind him when he left the office. He wanted to have a real weekend for once. Two entire days where the pressures of work didn't fog his mind and capture his attention.

Eventually, Quinn peeled his eyes away from the screen. As he looked away, his vision still saw data patterns and spreadsheets. He needed a walk.

Tossing his third cup of coffee into the trash, he walked through the hallway to the coffee stand for another drink. Espresso. No need for anything but caffeine.

As Quinn approached the coffee stand, he saw someone standing casually, chatting with the barista. The man didn't look familiar, but he looked too patient for Quinn's liking. The man just stood there, nonchalantly talking back and forth with the person who was supposed to be expediently taking orders and pouring coffee drinks. Quinn couldn't decide if the man had even ordered a drink yet.

Growing more and more impatient, Quinn finally stepped up

to the stand.

"Excuse me," Quinn said. "I don't mean to interrupt, but I need an espresso. Like, now."

The barista shot a sideways glance at Quinn, transfiguring his face into one of obligatory customer service.

"Coming right up, sir," the barista said.

Soon enough, the barista handed the espresso to Quinn, who turned away and dashed back to his office without a word.

As he returned to his chair, a feeling of remorse dug into his lungs.

I was so rude to that guy, Quinn thought. *What am I doing?*

As Quinn dove into his spreadsheets. The thought evaporated, along with the feeling of remorse. The morning swiftly transformed into afternoon. Quinn felt lighter as he watched the sun dip behind the city's skyscrapers again. The late afternoon sun, paired with his dwindling to-do list, gave Quinn a bit of relief.

He had plans to meet an old college friend for a drink downtown. Maybe he could enjoy a Friday night in the city without the concerns of work weighing him down.

The concept intrigued him. Checking his watch, he began to reach for his briefcase to pack up for the weekend.

Then, he heard a knock on his door, which was already open. Turning to look, he saw his boss standing there with a determined expression.

"Quinn," the boss said, "the board just ran the numbers and they look good. We'll need a full strategy map on my desk by tomorrow evening."

Quinn's heart sank.

"Tomorrow's Saturday, sir," Quinn said.

"That's never stopped you before," the boss said. "You're a worker, Mr. Thomas. That's what I like about you."

He nodded to emphasize the compliment. Quinn fumed, but attempted to maintain a calm exterior.

"And just know that your efforts will be rewarded," the boss said, turning toward the door. "With your new role and increased dedication to the company, you'll see a massive salary increase. And a nice bonus at the end of the year."

The boss stopped in the doorway and returned his attention to Quinn.

"A penthouse downtown and a new sports car are within your grasp," the boss said. "But if you can't get it done…"

With that, he left Quinn's office and powered through the hallway.

Quinn sunk into his chair. The sun painted the sky. Skyscrapers reflected with gold. Unbuttoning his collar, he loosened his tie and looked blankly out the window.

A piercing headache forced his eyes shut. Suddenly, he became aware of the jackhammer far below his office, and the screeching of construction equipment near his building. The air conditioning fan seemed to throb throughout the room. And then, the walls closed in and his vision darkened.

Breathing heavily and methodically, Quinn calmed himself. These stress-related attacks had happened before, but lately, they seemed to be occurring more frequently.

As he regained his vision and composure, he looked at his desk calendar and realized he had forgotten to eat lunch again. In fact, he had neglected to drink water as well. Coffee fueled him with false energy and suppressed hunger.

Standing from his desk, he grabbed his briefcase and left his office. He was chronically late to any appointment that did not relate to work; Quinn did not want to make that a habit.

He sped through the hallway. He did not want his bosses and

board members to see him leaving work on time; that would reflect poorly on his reputation at the office. Finally, he made it across the Pit and to the elevators.

One drink with Charlie, Quinn thought, *then I'm back to the office to work through the night.*

Chapter 3

Quinn elbowed his way toward the train door as his stop approached. His briefcase hung over his shoulder; he clutched it to prevent another pickpocket experience. The doors opened and Quinn flowed onto the platform with the crowd, shuffling toward the staircase. The smell of urine and trash wafted through the corridor. Muffled footsteps echoed off the tiled walls.

It wasn't until Quinn emerged into the night air that he released a full exhale. Letting his briefcase hang, he shoved his hands into his pockets as he strolled down the sidewalk. He watched a sports car speed away from its parking spot. The engine revved and the sound reverberated between the tall steel buildings, startling a few pedestrians. Its high beams flickered off skyscraper windows as it sped away.

A light rain began to fall, producing a shimmer from the streetlamps that lined the sidewalk. Quinn approached the building and nodded to the doorman, who opened the door to the restaurant.

High rollers dotted tables throughout the open floor. Quinn saw Charlie sitting at the bar near the back of the restaurant and began to move that way, but the host held up a gloved hand. Straightening his tie as he approached Quinn, the host eyed the reservation menu on the table.

"Reservation, sir?" the host asked.

"No," Quinn said. "Just meeting a friend for a drink. I see him back there already."

The host glared at Quinn. Evidently, Quinn passed the test. The host stepped aside and motioned for Quinn to walk toward the bar.

The metallic bar prioritized modernism over comfort. Dark shadows contrasted with light beams and oddly placed mirrors. Liquor bottles beamed, lining the illuminated back wall.

Charlie stood from his stool at the bar and shook Quinn's hand before motioning for Quinn to sit next to him.

"What's up, Charlie?" Quinn said.

"Good to see you, Quinn," Charlie said. "What are you drinking tonight?"

Quinn scanned the drink menu. Though he had hoped for a beer list, the drink menu seemed to feature nothing but elaborate cocktails.

The bartender approached and Quinn ordered a manhattan.

"Classic choice," Charlie said. "I elected to sip on a scotch that the bartender had to pull from their private collection."

Quinn feigned interest.

"What have you been up to, man?" Quinn asked. "I haven't seen you in months."

Charlie smirked, sipped his scotch, and placed his glass down on the bar.

"It has been a wild few months," Charlie said. "Share prices at my firm are through the roof, largely because of my initiatives and protocol restructuring."

Quinn nodded. He saw the bartender pour his manhattan on the other side of the bar.

"I heard from our secretary that our CEO has talked about bringing me in as an official partner in the firm," Charlie continued.

"That's exciting, man," Quinn said. "That was always the goal, right?"

"It sure was, but it's only the beginning," Charlie said. "It would be a nice stepping stone. Something to pacify me for the next few years, I suppose."

"Well, good for you, Charlie," Quinn said.

The bartender set the manhattan down in front of Quinn. As Quinn removed his credit card from his wallet, Charlie waved his hand.

"Drinks are on me tonight," Charlie said.

"Oh, don't even try," Quinn said. "We're celebrating your promotion. At the very least, I can get my own drinks."

Quinn's argument only fueled Charlie's pretentiousness.

"Well, thanks," Quinn said. "I'll get our drinks next time."

Charlie smirked and swirled his drink, feigning sophistication.

"With this work schedule I've adopted for myself, I don't know when that'll be," Charlie said. "Even though I have a penthouse downtown, I basically sleep at the office. I'm there every night until at least midnight. Up at five the next morning to gain an edge on our competition, of course."

"How are you holding up with all that?" Quinn asked.

"It takes its toll," Charlie said, "but it's worth it. I mean, you should see what they're paying me. It's what we always dreamed of!"

Quinn raised his glass halfway and leaned it toward Charlie, who reciprocated the gesture.

"How's Jenny?" Quinn asked. "Has she moved into your apartment yet?"

Charlie let out a laugh that echoed through the bar.

"Jenny couldn't handle my drive," Charlie said. "She tried to have a serious discussion with me about taking our commitment to the next level. She didn't like my response, so I allowed her to leave."

Quinn felt his spirit drop. He looked at Charlie with admiration for prioritizing business, but he also felt sorry for him. His drive was clouding his vision.

"I'm sorry, man," Quinn said.

Charlie laughed again. He sipped his scotch and swirled it around to experience its complexities.

"I'm not sorry," Charlie said. "Those are the necessary sacrifices that guys like you and me have to make if we want to make it to the top."

Quinn felt his stomach drop. As he took a drink of his manhattan, he caught his reflection in the barback mirror, but diverted his eyes to the liquor on the shelves.

Charlie tried to get the bartender's attention to order another drink. He looked at Quinn, hoping he would share in his own impatience.

"Hey, Charlie," Quinn said. "Do you ever feel like we're selling out?"

Snapping his attention away from the bartender, Charlie glared at Quinn.

"Not at all," Charlie said. "We're living the American Dream."

Charlie paused and waved to the bartender again. This time, he saw Charlie and walked over with the bottle of scotch.

"Well, at least *I'm* living the American Dream," Charlie said. "You're on your way, though."

"But are you *really* living the American Dream?" Quinn asked. "Think about it. What do we *actually* do? Create strategies and algorithms to help CEOs and companies get even richer than they already are."

Quinn finished his manhattan and pointed to the empty glass. The bartender nodded and began to make another one.

"And are we happy?" Quinn asked. "I know I certainly am not. I don't feel fulfilled at all in my job, even though I pour my heart and soul into it. I don't have any life outside of work, and my work is no kind of life."

"What are you? Some kind of Communist now?" Charlie asked.

Quinn shoved his face into his palms.

"No, I've just been thinking a lot lately about what kind of life I want to have," Quinn said. "And what kind of legacy I want to leave behind."

Charlie snatched his scotch from the bartender.

"What better legacy to leave behind than wealth and power," Charlie said.

* * *

Quinn finished his second drink. Charlie stood to leave. Quinn grabbed his briefcase and flung it over his shoulder. They walked through the restaurant and stepped out onto the street. The concrete was still wet from the rain, but the air was dry for the moment. Charlie handed his ticket to the valet, who sprinted down the sidewalk. A minute later, he drove a shiny green sports car around the corner and parked it in front of the restaurant.

"When did you get this?" Quinn asked.

"A few weeks ago," Charlie said. "Another perk of the American Dream."

Quinn shook his head.

"You'll be able to buy yourself one of these some day," Charlie said.

Charlie gave the valet a tip in exchange for the keys, and then shook Quinn's hand before sliding into his car.

"Good to see you," Quinn said.

"Good to see you, too," Charlie said. "Just keep climbing. You'll make it to the top soon enough."

Charlie smirked and closed his door. He revved the engine, spinning his tires on the wet pavement before darting into traffic.

Quinn turned and walked back down the sidewalk toward the subway. He didn't hear the crash.

Chapter 4

S treetlights burned through the darkness, guiding Quinn toward the steel skyscraper. Though cavernous, the entryway to Quinn's office building provided a sense of illumination, echoing back to the grandeur of a bygone era. With no one posted at the front desk, Quinn moved beyond the main room to the elevator corridor and took the ride to a higher level. Moving through the empty, darkened Pit, he found his office and flipped on the lights, evoking safety with a side of anxiety.

In some ways, Quinn enjoyed the solitude of the office at night. He had time to sit, to listen to the quiet hum of the city. But he wished he could be here to simply reflect, without the pressures of work projects or last-minute data analysis clouding his thoughts.

He tore through his computer files, setting up project folders, slideshows, and spreadsheets on separate monitors with ruthless efficiency. His heart pumped as his calendar alerted him of the pending due date for this project.

All he wanted to do was be home, to kick his feet up on the coffee table and watch the game. But work claimed his attention. Work always took first place.

A few blocks away, the large clock tower chimed.

9:00.

"Damn," Quinn said. "Already? I feel like I just got here."

His entire career rested on the success and turnaround of this project. He needed this promotion. If he wanted to compete with Charlie, he needed the salary that came with it. And the social status. With this new position and recognition, Quinn knew he would be grabbing casual drinks with some of the city's biggest names and most recognizable faces.

But it all depended on this project, a project he thought he would have months to complete. And now, his boss needed it in less than a day. This wasn't what Quinn signed up for. Or was it?

Feeling himself being absorbed into his screen, he stood and walked around his small office to move blood through his veins, to feel a little bit alive. Returning to his chair, he honed in on his project screens.

The clock tower chimed again.

10:00.

Quinn slammed his forehead into his desk. He felt like he was making no progress on this project.

He decided to take a short break and catch up on some financial news before tomorrow's investment cycle began. Swiping through his usual newspapers and financial guides, Quinn landed on the city's major current event paper.

And then he saw it. The headline read *Financial Manager Dead in Head-on Collision.*

Quinn's heartbeat quickened. He clicked on the article's headline. He clicked again. It wasn't loading fast enough. Part of him didn't want the article to load.

But when it did, Quinn's heart sank.

Charles Jacobson was declared dead on impact after a head-on collision with a semi truck in Midtown on Friday night. Early reports indicate that the semi truck driver fell asleep at the wheel and drove into opposing traffic, causing the fatal collision.

That was all Quinn could read. His hand began to twitch, and then his face. His peripheral vision started to darken, accompanied by a blurred sensation. Breathing quickened. Sweat beaded. Heartbeat. Too fast.

Darkness.

* * *

When he lifted his head from his palms, he realized that he must have passed out.

This stress has to stop, he thought. *I can't handle this anymore.*

Quinn stood and cracked open a water bottle, splashing water on his hands and rubbing the caked sweat from his face. He dried the droplets and moved back toward his desk.

His computer screen had gone black, unused for too long. Quinn caught his own ghostly reflection on the screen.

And then he saw him.

But just for a moment.

I'm going crazy, Quinn thought. *I'm seeing dead people on my computer.*

Frantic, Quinn illuminated his computer screen to erase the mental image of Charlie in the reflection. But the feeling of darkness remained. Out the window, Quinn saw a black cloud gather in the distance. A gust of wind swept off the water and cut through the streets.

Go, the wind said.

Quinn's eyes scanned the room. He knew he was going crazy. Having some sort of work-induced, panic-stricken mental breakdown.

Go, the voice echoed.

"Charlie?" Quinn said.

Quinn looked around the room, investigating the shadowy corners of his office. He stood from his desk and looked out the window into the cityscape. Car lights and traffic signals shifted, creating a light show far below. And then Charlie's reflection appeared in the window.

Quinn's heart pounded. He spun around to face the reflection. But he saw no one. Just an empty office.

He returned his attention to the reflection in the window, but all he saw was himself staring back. Frightened, Quinn returned to his desk and sat.

The clock tower outside struck 11:00 and snapped Quinn from his daze. Looking into the darkened office floor, Quinn saw a figure moving through the Pit. Quinn's heart rate spiked. His hands began to shake with adrenaline.

The figure moved toward the edge of the cubicle maze and flipped on the lights in a corner office. After a few deep breaths, rationality returned to Quinn's mind.

My boss is here this late on a Friday, Quinn thought. *Weird*.

As Quinn glared at his computer screens again, a feeling of assertion overcame him. Looking around for some form of reassurance, he stood up with intention. He filled his briefcase with necessary personal items and charged through the door into the hallway, maneuvering his way through the Pit to the only other illuminated room on the floor.

"Hey, boss," Quinn said, posting himself in the door frame.

"Mr. Thomas," the boss said, "I thought I might see you here. Working on that strategy map, I presume?"

"I was, sir," Quinn said.

The boss nodded, though his attempt at conveying approval came across as a sign of patronizing control. Quinn felt a familiar restlessness arise.

"I'm just here to grab my tickets," the boss said. "I get to take our clients to the big game tonight. In our corporate suite, of course."

Quinn's eyebrows narrowed.

"Some day, maybe you'll even get an invitation to an event like this," the boss said. "If you keep putting in long hours and show yourself as dedicated to this company as your only priority, you can be like me."

The boss finished his statement with a grin. He grabbed his tickets off of his desk and slipped them into his suit jacket pocket. As he moved toward the door, he hesitated, recognizing that he could not bypass Quinn's frame in the doorway.

"You know, I'm not sure if that's what I want anymore," Quinn said.

He shifted his weight to the other foot.

"I just don't know if I can dedicate my whole life to this office," Quinn said. "Life's too short."

The boss stepped backward and narrowed his eyes.

"Mr. Thomas," the boss said, "I'm surprised to hear you say that. I always took you for a go-getter. Someone with true ambition."

Quinn smiled and crossed his arms.

"I have ambition, sir," Quinn said. "I just can't direct my ambition to this hectic, anxiety-driven lifestyle anymore."

The boss frowned. He stepped toward Quinn.

"What are you saying, Mr. Thomas?" the boss said.

Quinn smiled again. His nerves shook, but something within his soul felt alive. More alive than it had in years.

"I quit, sir," Quinn said. "Consider this conversation my official resignation."

The boss's jaw dropped open. His eyebrows shot up. Quinn sped through the Pit and burst through the door to the stairway. He skipped alternating steps as he dashed to the ground level.

He gasped for breath and wiped sweat from his forehead as he moved into the lobby. A few iridescent lights paved the way to the glass doors.

Once outside, he stopped and breathed in the cool night air. He allowed the air to fill his lungs, to rejuvenate his body. A light rain fell from the sky. Streetlight streaks caught rain droplets and sparkled. Quinn walked underneath the mist, allowing it to cleanse him.

People emerged from the subway and crowded the sidewalk; their footsteps echoed in puddles. Chatter filled vacant spaces in the air.

Quinn climbed the apartment building stairs two at a time. Lucy sat on the couch watching television, but diverted her attention when she heard Quinn unlock the door.

"I did it!" Quinn shouted.

Lucy analyzed Quinn.

"Good for you!" she said. "What did you do, exactly?"

Quinn smiled and plopped on the couch next to her.

"I finally quit my job," he said.

Lucy shot backwards. A look of disgust crossed her face, followed by a forced expression of support.

"Interesting," Lucy said. "Why did you do that?"

Quinn felt a lump begin to well up in his throat. He covered his face with his hands as he held back tears.

"Charlie's dead," Quinn said.

"Who's Charlie?" Lucy asked.

Quinn looked at her. Really looked at her. His eyebrows narrowed as he tried to decipher her capacity for empathy.

"Seriously, Quinn," she said. "Was Charlie your family dog or something?"

"No!" Quinn said. "Charlie is my...was my friend from college. I've been friends with him for ten years. We met freshman year. And now he's just...gone."

Lucy got up and walked to the kitchen. She grabbed a soda from the refrigerator and stood near the kitchen table.

"If you were such good friends with this guy, how come I never met him?" Lucy asked.

Quinn raised an eyebrow as he turned toward her.

"Are you serious?" he said.

"All I'm saying is that if he was such a good friend, you'd think I would have met him," Lucy said. "You're just being dramatic. You're just trying to get sympathy from me so I won't make you feel like an idiot for quitting your job."

Quinn's stomach dropped. He felt his face flush, his pulse quicken. Beads of sweat started to form on his forehead.

"He was probably one of those business connections that you take so much pride in collecting," Lucy said. "You don't even have real friends."

"Charlie *was* a real friend," Quinn said. "I knew him for a long time."

Lucy rolled her eyes.

"And besides, he was going to help me follow his lead," Quinn said. "He was going to guide me toward rising in my own company. Toward building a serious business portfolio for myself. Toward building a serious financial future for you and me."

Lucy threw her head back and laughed.

"For *us*?" Lucy said. "There is no us. There should be an us. But you spend so much time focused on work and rising to the top that you barely even acknowledge my existence."

"Are you serious right now?" Quinn shouted. "I go out with you and your friends all the time."

"Physically, you're there," Lucy said. "But you're never *actually* present. You spend so much time focusing on making money that you never have the presence to focus on me."

Quinn threw his arms up in the air and started to pace the floor.

"Don't you want to have a secure life?" Quinn asked. "Don't you want to live in a big house with a nice car? Don't you want a husband who allows you to spend carefree days doing whatever makes you happy?"

"That's your problem, Quinn," Lucy said. "You have such a flawed definition of happiness. I want to get married to *you*, not your money. I want to start a family with *you*, not your title. I want to spend my life with *you*, not just occupy the same space."

He forced back the lump in his throat as he stood and faced Lucy.

"What?" Lucy said. "Nothing to say?"

"It's time for you to leave," Quinn said.

Lucy rolled her eyes.

"Are you serious?" Lucy asked.

Quinn dropped his head and attempted to control his breathing.

"Lucy, go home," Quinn said.

"So, I guess this means we're not going to move in together next month?" she said.

"It would probably be better for both of us if you didn't come back," Quinn said.

"You need to make a change," she said. "Not for me, but for yourself."

Lucy snatched her purse off the kitchen table and stomped toward the door. As she grasped the knob, she turned and looked Quinn in the eye.

"Or, maybe you're right," Lucy said. "Maybe you really are nothing but a paycheck."

She slammed the door behind her. Quinn stood in his apartment, alone in the silence.

Chapter 5

Quinn fit his backpack into the overhead compartment, cramming it between the plastic siding and another passenger's roller bag. He slid into the empty row and leaned against the window, hoping no one would take the middle seat next to him. He put his headphones on to dissuade any overly cheerful passengers from engaging in frivolous chatter. The headphones weren't connected to anything, but they dulled the noise.

He opened his book and started reading, but was forced to pause when the plane's crew crackled over the loudspeaker to welcome all passengers aboard. After the slightly entertaining safety routine speech, Quinn returned to his book.

The plane taxied to the runway. No one had taken the middle seat. As the plane rose, Quinn peered through the window and watched the skyscrapers and familiarity fade away.

He read. He slept. He read some more. He looked at his one-way ticket, wondering if had been crazy for making such a spontaneous decision to leave the country. He changed planes in Mexico City.

Quinn watched in awe as the plane flew above the Andes Mountains. The jagged peaks towered above the clouds below, creating snow-capped islands in the sky.

Gazing out the window, Quinn caught a shimmer in the reflection.

Charlie, Quinn thought.

"*Perdón, Señor*," a flight attendant said.

Quinn jolted from his daze.

"We're about to make our descent into Cusco," the flight attendant continued. "Please lift your tray table into the upright position."

Quinn nodded and complied. The flight attendant smiled and continued down the aisle.

Eventually, the plane descended into a valley. Surrounded by mountain peaks, houses packed themselves into the natural bowl. Quinn saw narrow mazes of alleyways that darted between compact buildings. The sun began to set behind the mountains, replaced by the moon that hung above the city.

"*Bienvenidos a Cusco*," the captain said over the loudspeaker. "We hope you enjoy your time in Peru."

Quinn grabbed his backpack and strolled down the aisle. He bumped into an older woman with his backpack and muttered a nervous *lo siento*. The Spanish phrase fluttered with a heavy American accent, a result of linguistic rust. Quinn took Spanish in high school, but that was more than a decade ago. And he never used Spanish at the firm, not when he was surrounded by English-speaking, insulated white Americans.

As he stepped out of the plane, Quinn felt a sense of panic overcome his nerves. He was not familiar with this airport, or this style, or this culture. This was not an airport in Chicago or New York or Seattle. This was another country. Another way of life. And that realization swept over him like a wave.

Stepping through the airport's sliding doors, he waved at a stationary taxi, which sped to the curbside. An older man emerged and nodded to Quinn. He said something in Spanish, but it was too fast for Quinn's untrained ear to comprehend. The man pointed to Quinn's backpack and held out his hands, so Quinn removed his pack and gave it to the driver, who tossed the bag in the trunk. Quinn sat in the back seat.

"*Hablas español?*" the driver asked.

"*Un poco,*" Quinn said.

"No problem," the driver said in Spanish. "Where to?"

Quinn showed the driver a printed name of a hostel. The driver nodded and sped away from the airport curb.

The driver navigated sparse traffic with precision. Looking out the window, Quinn saw the city of Cusco emerge. Houses made of wood and stone smashed against each other, creating compact cobblestone alleyways and narrow streets. Colorful markets and populated plazas bustled with people. Mountains rose above the city in all directions.

As the driver weaved through cars into an alleyway, Quinn's breath quickened. A familiar sense of anxiety began to flood his vision. And he knew the cause of this anxiety wave: this was the first time he had left the United States. This was culture shock.

* * *

Quinn tossed his backpack onto the table and sat on the single bed in his room. Resisting the temptation to crash onto his sheets and sleep, he rose and followed the tile flooring onto the balcony out his front door. Two floors of rooms bordered a small, open-air courtyard. As he looked up, he saw more stars than he had ever seen in the city back home. A few guests wandered through the courtyard, speaking a language that Quinn recognized as neither English nor Spanish. Acting on a sudden urge to be anywhere other than his room, he trotted down the stairs and left the hostel.

It was still early in the evening, but the environment was dark. A few orange streetlights dotted the narrow road, a stark difference from the perpetually illuminated cities in the States. He threw on his sweatshirt to block the slight chill. It was winter in the Southern Hemisphere.

Quinn trekked downhill, careful to mind his footing on the uneven stone sidewalk. With no destination in mind, Quinn emerged from the thin street and walked toward a large plaza.

He paused and leaned against an old stone wall to catch his breath. He was not in prime physical condition anymore, but his short downhill walk should not have been this strenuous. Cusco's 11,000-foot elevation was taking its toll on Quinn's lungs.

In the dark, winter night, the plaza buzzed with light and chatter. Loud drum beats echoed from a staircase leading to a stone church. Teenagers danced in a circle, their steps in unison with the drum beat.

Quinn saw an older man walk by and decided to ask him about the dancing. His curiosity overrode his nervous Spanish.

"What's going on over there?" Quinn asked.

"Practice," the man said.

Quinn understood the Spanish phrase, but not the context.

"Practice for what?" Quinn asked.

"*Inti Raymi*," the man said. "The Festival of the Sun. It's a tradition that happens around the Winter Solstice. It dates back to when the Inca ruled Cusco."

Quinn smiled. His face conveyed interest.

"It connects us to our ancestors, our rich heritage as people of Cusco," the man continued.

A curious smile appeared on the man's face.

"According to legend," the man continued, "during *Inti Raymi*, the ghosts of the ancestors appear to those who need it. The walk alongside us. They guide us on our journey to a better life."

The man's face remained stoic. Quinn raised an eyebrow, causing the man to break his expression into laughter.

"The festival isn't for another week, but stick around," the man said. "You'll enjoy it."

Quinn nodded and thanked the old man, who smiled and dissipated into the crowd.

The crowd seemed to engulf Quinn too. He felt his anxiety close its grip. The crowd was too large, too constricting. He didn't understand the language, the purpose. All the buildings were too old, too many stories with histories that Quinn didn't yet understand.

But something about the crowd drew him in. Everyone seemed connected, somehow pulled by the same energy, the same focus. Maybe they were fused together by a shared history, a shared culture, a shared desire to simultaneously connect with the past and the present.

He watched as the dancers swirled together in a blur, blending with the ancient buildings and stone-paved streets. He felt enchanted, caught in a mysterious trance.

A young man bumped into him, snapping Quinn from his daze. The man was shorter than Quinn. Maybe five years younger. Quinn apologized and the man waved it off with a smile, returning to his group of friends, who stood watching the dancers practice their ancient choreography.

The dancers swung around with feathers and headgear, stand-ins for the real event in a few days. The drum beat drove the dance steps. And it drove the group of friends next to Quinn to sing in Spanish.

The young man looked over at Quinn and motioned for him to join the circle. This time, Quinn waved him off, smiling as a polite decline of the offer. But the group insisted, pushing Quinn to the forefront of the small group.

Nervous, Quinn sang a little. His voice was quiet and nervous. But he did it. And his voice grew slightly more confident as he sang. He didn't know the words, but he picked up the chorus soon enough. The friends cheered him on. Quinn sang louder, matching the volume of the group. He was out of his comfort zone.

Temporarily, Quinn felt like he was part of something larger, something that had a purpose. Somehow, he understood the significance of this song and its power.

And, just as quickly, that understanding vanished.

Quinn continued his walk through the plaza, through the crowd. He passed the front of a Spanish colonial cathedral; its bell towers loomed, tall and foreboding. Quinn kept walking to the center of the plaza. As he looked up, he saw a golden statue of Tupac Amaru that stood above the center of the plaza, a symbol of the Inca's last stand against their Spanish invaders.

Quinn thought about his own Spanish heritage. He wasn't too familiar with it; it was a distant history. He only knew the stories that his mother had told him when he was younger. Stories that may have morphed into legend, containing half-truths and concealment. But Quinn couldn't shake the feeling that, a long time ago, one of his own ancestors likely invaded a civilization like this one, invading with thoughts of greed and power, or material wealth and personal advancement.

Has anything really changed? Quinn thought.

As he looked at the statue again, he couldn't help but feel like Tupac Amaru was reprimanding him. Like he was somehow forcing Quinn to wrestle with his own past.

On the other side of the plaza, the dancers began to ring bells and bang drums, sending an echo between the Inca ruins and the colonial churches, reverberating the stone beneath Quinn's feet. The language, the chatter, the history, the conflict, the culture. The chains around Quinn's mind loosened.

Chapter 6

Quinn needed coffee. Fast. He threw on his clothes and walked out of his room. Crossing the courtyard of the old hacienda, he saw all of the hostel doors still closed. The sun had begun to shine light on the courtyard through the open roof, but the morning felt brisk. Nodding to the young woman at the front desk, Quinn left the safety of the hostel and walked onto the uneven cobblestone sidewalk.

He allowed gravity to do most of the work, moving downhill toward the central plaza. He passed small corner stores, still closed with metal security gates. He kept walking.

Quinn ran his hand along a stone wall as he walked. He paused for a minute and admired the perfectly cut stone. Examining it closer, he realized just how precise these stones were. He remembered something he read on the airplane about Inca architecture, something about the stone being cut so perfectly that they did not need adhesive. Something about architectural perfection without beasts of burden or the use of the wheel. Something about how Inca buildings weathered the barrage of earthquakes in the Andes better than modern buildings did. Something about how their methods remained a mystery.

A few food carts began to set up on their usual corners. Stray dogs trotted from alleyways and hiding spots to claim their territory next to their most loyal food vendors.

The sky brightened as the sun rose above the mountain bowl that encircled Cusco; sun rays glistened off of the golden Tupac Amaru statue in the center of the plaza, which remained otherwise empty.

Craving something less familiar, Quinn continued through the plaza and turned down an alleyway. Finally, he encountered a coffee shop that looked alive. A bell rang as Quinn opened the door. He waved to the old woman behind the counter.

"*Buenos días*," Quinn said.

"Good morning," she said. "What would you like?"

Quinn ordered a coffee and a pastry. He was the first customer of the day; the woman made his coffee and pulled a fresh pastry from the oven. It was still too warm to eat. Quinn thanked her and found a seat outside.

The small table sat unevenly on the cobblestone streetside. Slightly bothered by the table's wobble, Quinn attempted to ignore the imperfection. He focused his attention on the way that Cusco woke up. Shops opened slowly. Business owners took their time. They shouted friendly greetings to their neighbors, even pausing their own opening to discuss last night's soccer game. Couples and families strolled down the alleyway. Only a few people mosied into Quinn's coffee shop, and the owner did not mind that perceived lack of business. She stood patiently at the counter and read the newspaper.

Quinn couldn't help but notice the stark contrast between Cusco and his own culture back home in the States, a culture that took pride in its motivation to ignore other human beings and focus solely on money and hurry.

Finishing his coffee, Quinn left the coffee shop and continued to wander through alleyways and side streets. He had no plan, no destination in mind. He just wanted to experience something different.

A stray dog followed him as he strolled down a bright street. Loud voices and honking cars echoed around the corner, so Quinn followed the noise. He came to a large open-air market-place that occupied an entire city block.

This is different, Quinn thought.

He pushed into the market and saw hundreds of people flocked together, moving with the crowd. Dozens of narrow pathways weaved between shops and stands, each one full of bright colors, patterned fabrics, and loud chatter in Spanish and Quechua. Alpaca wool sweaters, knit caps, backpacks, table clothes. The bartering between customers and shop owners seemed rehearsed, like a well-choreographed dance.

And then Quinn smelled the food area of the market. Fresh fruits, sauteed vegetables, grilled meat. Quinn didn't need to eat, but the food smelled too good to pass up. He stepped to a food cart and ordered a plate of whatever they served. He received a seemingly basic plate of beef, rice, and vegetables. He wandered to a community table and dove into the simple, delicious plate.

An older man sat across from Quinn and placed a coffee and a newspaper on the table. He nodded to Quinn before lighting a cigarette.

"How do you like the food?" the man asked in Spanish.

"It's amazing," Quinn said.

The man smiled and sipped his coffee. Smoke from the end of his cigarette swirled around his wide-brimmed hat.

"You're not from Cusco," the man asked. "What brings you here?"

"Great question," Quinn said. "I really don't know."

The man scrunched his face.

"You don't know why you came to Cusco?" the man asked.

Quinn stuck his fork into the pile of rice.

"Not really," he said. "I wasn't finding happiness in the States. I guess I just needed a change."

"It's always good to pursue happiness and fulfillment," the man said. "How do you plan to find fulfillment in Peru?

Quinn smiled at the simplicity of the question.

"I hadn't really thought that far ahead," Quinn said. "I booked a ticket to somewhere that seemed different from my home city, and that was the extent of my plan."

The man nodded and took a long drag from his cigarette. As he exhaled, the smoke circled around his hat brim and disappeared into the air above his head.

"You know Machu Picchu?" the man asked.

"I think I've heard of it," Quinn said.

The man nodded slowly.

"Machu Picchu is an ancient Incan city that sits on top of a steep mountain," the man said. "When the Spanish invaded Peru, they destroyed as much of Incan culture as they could. But the city of Machu Picchu was so high above the river below that the Spanish never found it. It remained well-preserved for centuries."

Quinn's eyes widened. He leaned forward, resting his elbows against the table.

"The trek to Machu Picchu," the man said, "is long and difficult. It takes five days on foot and climbs up and down the jagged peaks of the Andes Mountains. It leads adventurers through barren deserts, frozen glaciers, and the edges of the Amazon jungle. It takes people through unbearable altitude and pushes the limits of the human condition."

He paused and took another drag of his cigarette, exhaling smoke as he spoke.

"A journey to Machu Picchu," the man said, "is not something you can complete alone. You'll make the journey with other adventurers who seek some sort of purpose, some sort of higher calling. And, through this journey together, you just might find what you're searching for."

The man extinguished his cigarette in an ashtray. He grabbed his newspaper and coffee as he stood, nodding to Quinn one last time before disappearing into the marketplace crowd.

* * *

The sun hung high above the city as Quinn weaved through its maze of side streets. His lungs burned from the long walk in high altitude, but he pushed forward. Finally, he found the door. He wiped sweat from his forehead as he approached the front desk.

"Hello, sir," the man at the front desk said. "How can I help you?"

"I'd like to trek to Machu Picchu," Quinn said.

The man frowned and looked at Quinn with sympathy.

"I'm sorry, sir," the man said, "but treks to Machu Picchu must be scheduled months in advance."

Quinn's heart sank. He rested his arms against the desk and felt his inspiration leave his body.

"You know," the man said, "let me check our schedule. Sometimes people have to cancel their treks at the last minute and we can't fill their spot. Hold on a minute."

The man sifted through the calendar on his computer. Quinn wanted to remain optimistic, but he didn't want his hopes to deflate again, so he maintained his skepticism.

Then, the man's eyebrows lifted. He turned to Quinn.

"We have an open spot!" he shouted. "A five-day trek to Machu Picchu."

"That's great news!" Quinn said. "When does it start?"

The man smirked.

"Tomorrow morning at 4:00 a.m."

Chapter 7

Orange street lights flickered underneath the dark sky, creating shadows in foreboding alleyways. Quinn clutched his backpack and swiveled his head back and forth in an effort to remain vigilant. He had arrived on the street corner at 3:45 a.m. and the frigid mountain air began to take control of Quinn's nerves.

The van arrived 18 minutes late. It honked and flashed its headlights as it lumbered around the narrow street corner.

The driver emerged from the van and grabbed Quinn's backpack and tossed it in the vehicle's overhead storage compartment.

"*Gracias*," Quinn grumbled.

The driver slid the van's side door open. Quinn saw seven figures, seven shadows seated throughout the van. Some slept against the window, while some stared at Quinn. A wave of self-consciousness overtook Quinn as he jumped into the vehicle. He took the last open seat in the middle row near the door. Before he had secured his seat belt, the van sped away, weaving through another side street.

"*La ultima persona?*" the driver asked.

"*Si,*" the navigator said.

They finished their logistics and both looked straight ahead through the windshield. The engine's loud rumble echoed throughout the van's interior, which was otherwise silent. Strangers, shadowed faces, all on their way to the same location with the same sense of adventure.

Quinn looked out the window and watched the old stone city speed through his vision, obscured by darkness and blurred by unfamiliarity.

Eventually, the van merged onto a faster street that took the group out of Cusco. The engine revved as it climbed a mountain pass. Spaced street lights shot moments of light into the van, reflecting off of passenger faces before concealing them again in darkness. Quinn looked around, careful not to draw attention to himself.

The man in the front seat looked like many of the men he had seen walking around Cusco: dark features, small in stature, and a sense of contentment. He nodded at the radio, which hummed with sports commentary in rapid Spanish, too quick for Quinn to catch.

Quinn glanced over his shoulder and saw a young man, possibly of South Asian descent, leaning against the window, pretending to sleep to pass the time. His long black hair was tied into a bun, and his clothes suggested that he was well-traveled.

The man next to Quinn was awake, but quiet. His dark skin and buzzed hair were visible in the sparse light as he looked out the window and watched the mountains awaken. The man held an Ivory Coast passport in his hand.

The woman in the back row was asleep against the window. Her white skin contrasted with her black hair, which was tied with a bandana in the colors of the Spanish flag. She had a camera strapped to her shoulder.

The other figures on the bus were too concealed in darkness

46

for Quinn to spy, so he decided to return his attention to the sparse scenery out his window. He saw a few houses dot the roadside, lit only by porch lights.

His thoughts traveled to Lucy. Quinn doubted she would wait for him to have a change of heart, to return to his high-paying career.

But maybe I should go back, Quinn thought.

A shimmer flashed across Quinn's reflection in the window. He wondered what Charlie would have thought about this spontaneous trip to a foreign country's most prized location.

He'd think I was crazy, Quinn thought. *A waste of time and money. I should be focusing on work to reach the next level.*

The image of Charlie's sports car sped across Quinn's mind. A sudden feeling of conviction filled Quinn's soul.

Or maybe Charlie would think I'm exactly right, Quinn thought. *Maybe this is the change Charlie needed but never got.*

He paused his thought trail and focused through the glass.

Maybe this is Charlie's way of atonement, he thought.

Eventually, the road weaved into a narrow mountain pass that brought the van to the edge of a river. The van slowed, and then came to a complete stop. The Peruvian man from the front seat jumped out and slid the van door open. He tossed each passenger their backpack as they filed into the cold morning air. The sun had started its climb above the mountains, but light was still thin.

"Alright team," the Peruvian man said in Spanish. "Gather around."

The group of eight huddled together in front of him. Each person seemed equally uncomfortable.

The group was already behind schedule, driving a sense of anxiety through Quinn's mind, a product of habit from his school and work training.

"Welcome to the start of your journey," the Peruvian man said. "My name is Antonio, and I will be your trail guide along our journey to Machu Picchu."

"*Buenos días, Antonio,*" the Spanish woman said.

Antonio nodded in response.

"We'll begin our first day of trekking in a few minutes, but first, we need to set some rules," Antonio said.

The trekkers looked around, trying to get a feel for the other members in the group.

"First, have fun," Antonio said. "Get to know each other. We'll be hiking for five days, so it's important that you get to know your new friends. We have people in our group from five different continents, all with the same goal of exploring history, so talk with one another. Learn."

Quinn looked around at the faces of each group member, all different, all equally filled with the spark of adventure.

"Second, stay close to the group," Antonio continued. "We don't want anyone to get lost in the Andes or the Amazon. If you feel tired from the climb, let me know and we can make adjustments. I hope you packed light."

Quinn lifted his backpack from the ground and strapped it to his shoulders. Its weight made him doubt his decision to hike.

"Third, we will hike for about ten hours each day," Antonio said. "That means early mornings so we can stop to rest and eat before the sun sets. The scenery is beautiful and diverse, just like all of you. So, are you ready to take the journey to Machu Picchu?"

A few of the group members nodded slowly. Antonio shook his head.

"Are you ready to take the journey to Machu Picchu?" Antonio shouted.

"Yeah!" the man from the Ivory Coast shouted.

Quinn followed his example and shouted too. Somehow, the collective shout put Quinn at ease. He felt a familiar pressure to impress the people around him. But, somehow, that pressure was beginning to dissipate.

Antonio whipped his hand in the air and turned toward the mountain. Stepping onto the path, he began to walk. Quinn looked around at the other group members, who returned his glance with equal confusion. Slowly, Quinn clutched his backpack straps and took a step, following Antonio down the path. The other group members did the same.

The adventure had begun.

* * *

The first mile pushed Quinn uphill through low bushes coated in morning dew. The sun climbed the mountain peaks that surrounded the trekking group in all directions. Lined with vegetation on one side, the single-person trail edged a steep drop on the other, producing a perpetual sense of fear through Quinn's unsteady legs. With Antonio in the lead, Quinn followed in silence.

At 10,000 feet above sea level, the crisp morning air felt frigid, but that did not prevent sweat from drenching Quinn's hair. His lungs burned. His throat closed with thirst. Looking over his shoulder, he saw the rest of the group following him, maintaining the fast pace with seeming ease. Quinn was too embarrassed to stop for a drink; they had only been walking for an hour.

Luckily, Antonio stopped and stood on the side of the trail, away from the ledge. He motioned for the group to stop as well.

"How are we all feeling?" Antonio asked.

His breath was even, not even a drop of perspiration on his forehead.

"I'm exhausted," a woman shouted in Spanish from the back of the line.

"Doing great," a man said. "Hardly broke a sweat."

Antonio looked at Quinn. With nothing but a smile and a nod, Antonio recognized Quinn's struggle.

Quinn took a red bandana from his backpack and wrapped it around his head to catch the sweat that continued to pour.

"Drink some water," Antonio said to the group. "It's important to keep hydrated this high up."

Quinn snatched his water bottle from the side of his pack and chugged. He felt refreshed, but the burning in his lungs had been replaced with fire in his legs. Sure, he was at altitude, but his daily routine of fried food, soda, and sitting had not prepared him for the physical toll of extreme trekking.

"In a few hours, we'll stop at 13,000 feet to set up camp. It's a short day today. We need to get you acclimated to the altitude."

"I'm sorry," Quinn said. "We're camping two and half miles above sea level?"

Antonio threw his head back and laughed.

"Welcome to the Andes, *amigo*," Antonio said.

The small group finished their break and continued to climb the trail. Each step brought Quinn higher in elevation and closer to collapse.

An hour had passed since he last drank water, since he allowed his legs to be still. He struggled to inhale each breath as he passed the 11,000-foot mark.

He tried to force the idea of quitting from his mind. But the thought had supplanted itself, taking control of Quinn's legs. Finally, he stopped and sat on a rock.

Antonio noticed Quinn's pause and encouraged the rest of the group to take a break. As other trekkers drank water, Antonio wandered over to Quinn.

"How are you feeling, my friend?" Antonio asked.

"I'm exhausted," Quinn said. "Honestly, I don't know if I can make it."

Antonio smiled and slapped Quinn on the shoulder.

"*Amigo*," Antonio said, "you can do anything you decide. If you want to quit, you can quit. But, if you want to trek to Machu Picchu, you can trek to Machu Picchu."

Quinn hung his head.

"No, Antonio," Quinn said, "I don't think my body will let me hike any farther."

"Trust me," Antonio said, "the human body can do incredible things. It's the human mind that gets in the way."

Quinn tilted his head and eyed Antonio, searching for meaning.

"What are you thinking about while you're hiking?" Antonio asked.

"Not much, I guess," Quinn said. "How hard it is to breathe. How exhausted my legs are."

"That's the problem," Antonio said. "Look around. You can't be thinking about yourself with all this natural beauty around."

Most of the trekkers had started placing their water bottles back in their packs. Some paced, clearly ready to continue the trek.

"I want you to try something," Antonio said. "As you hike, pay attention to what's around you. Pay attention to the way the landscape looks, and how the landscape changes. Focus on

51

the wind, the sun, the smell. Focus on the footsteps that have walked this ancient path before you. Soon enough, you'll be at camp."

"But..." Quinn said.

Antonio walked away and spun his arm above his head. The rest of the group followed Antonio as he continued up the narrow path. Startled, Quinn threw his pack on his shoulders and scampered to catch the group. Soon, the weight of his pack and the thin air brought the idea of quitting into Quinn's thoughts again.

A light breeze swept through the canyon, chilling the sweat in Quinn's hair. He surprised himself, noticing this detail, actually feeling this sentiment. For a second, he forgot his tired legs, his burning lungs.

He felt the sun warm his face through the cold mountain air. He smelled the highland vegetation as it rode on the breeze. The plants seemed thinner than they did at the beginning of the trek, shorter, more windswept. The grass and moss, coated in mountain dew, shifted the scent in the air.

Lifting his eyes from the trail, he noticed the mountains that rose in front of him. Their jagged sides met at distinct, majestic peaks.

Quinn's foot stepped on a stone, which brought his attention back to the trail. He was no longer walking on dirt. Before him, he saw a stone-paved path that weaved up the mountainside. He was walking on an ancient Inca trail, walking on the footsteps of history.

The whispers of Charlie's life floated in the breeze, a warning of a busy life left unfulfilled. Lucy echoed through Quinn's mind, spitting status-focused venom. The worry, the anxiety pushed Quinn forward.

And then, the group stopped. Quinn walked to the ledge of a rock and saw it: a turquoise lake, clear as glass, reflecting the magnitude of Salkantay's 20,000-foot snow-capped peak.

"We've made it to camp," Antonio said. "Good work, every-one!"

The group shouted and cheered. Quinn looked around, nervous. Catching Antonio's eye, Quinn decided to join in the celebration.

Antonio tossed his own pack to the ground and bowed his head in reverence.

Quinn did the same.

Chapter 8

The late afternoon sun had dipped below the mountains, which illuminated the sky, but dropped the temperature. Quinn crawled into his tent and grabbed a sweatshirt. His legs stiffened as he crouched.

He returned to the circle of stones that surrounded the fire pit. Most of the group continued to set up their tents and unpack their items for the night, so Quinn sat alone and absorbed the warmth of the fire.

Dry grass crunched below a pair of boots behind Quinn, which startled him. It was Antonio, who approached the fire pit and handed a mug of hot tea to Quinn.

"*Gracias*," Quinn said. "What is it?"

Antonio smiled.

"Coca tea," Antonio said. "The Andean people have been drinking this for centuries. It helps with altitude sickness, and it sharpens the mind."

Quinn sniffed his mug and took a drink. The tea warmed him. It tasted earthy. And maybe it helped the altitude-induced headache that was beginning to form above his ears.

"You know, the Inca used to run along this trail," Antonio said. "They used it as an information superhighway."

Quinn leaned forward. Coca tea steam wafted toward his nose.

"At the height of Inca rule," Antonio continued, "there were hundreds of miles of paved trails through the Andes. These trails connected all of the major Inca cities. And they all led back to Cusco."

"Did they ride horses along these trails?" Quinn asked.

"No, *amigo*," Antonio said. "The Inca did not use beasts of burden. Nor did they use the wheel. Messengers would run these trails from city to city to spread the news."

Quinn widened his eyes and nearly spit out his tea.

"People used to run these trails?" Quinn asked. "At 15,000 feet?"

"Yes they did," Antonio said. "The messengers were well-acclimated and possessed incredible levels of fitness."

"All to deliver letters?" Quinn asked.

Antonio sipped his tea and shook his head.

"Not to deliver mail," Antonio said. "The Inca did not utilize a system of writing. All of their messages and records were kept verbally, though they did use a system of colorful knots as a form of accounting."

Quinn's eyes followed the trail as it weaved through the mountains before disappearing over Salkantay Pass. With sore legs, he chugged his tea.

"How are you liking the journey so far?" Antonio continued in Spanish.

"It's alright," Quinn said.

Antonio raised an eyebrow and leaned forward again.

"I mean," Quinn continued, "the scenery is beautiful. But I don't think I'm cut out for this stuff. I'm not in great shape. And I don't know anybody here."

He hung his head and watched a coca tea leaf swirl around his mug.

"I would rather be back home in the comfort of the States," Quinn said. "At least I know my way around the city and the office. I've trained my body and mind to succeed in *that* environment."

Antonio shook his head. He held out his hand to stop Quinn from continuing his thought.

"Quinn, you can't give up yet," Antonio said. "You're embarking on the adventure of a lifetime. Stop thinking about what you're missing; focus on what you're gaining."

Quinn lifted his head from his swirling tea and focused on Antonio. Something about his sincerity drew Quinn's attention, fostering a trust that came without the need for time or personal experience.

"Home will always be there," Antonio continued, "but you won't always be here. I encourage you to be fully present. Push through the physical difficulty and enjoy the scenery. You Americans are so focused on work and money and schedules; this experience is about something else. Something bigger. Find out what that something is."

Grass crunched under another pair of boots behind the fire pit. Quinn turned to see the European woman and the African man walking toward the circle.

"And try opening up to some other trekkers," Antonio said. "You might learn something."

Antonio nodded toward the approaching trekkers as Quinn tried to hide his smile by sipping his empty tea cup.

Eventually, most of the trekking group members found their way to the circle around the fire pit. The smell of cooked vegetables and meat filled the air. The simplicity of the meal might have deterred Quinn a month ago, but it felt ideal for this environment. Soon enough, Antonio invited everyone to grab a plate and a drink.

Quinn sat on his stone and looked at the thick, yellow liquid that filled his cup. It felt cold in his palm. He smelled it. Pungent.

"Everyone grab your drink," Antonio said. "In your cup, we have a drink called *chicha*. It is an Andean beverage made from fermented corn. We have been making this drink since before Columbus arrived in the Caribbean. This drink has fueled celebrations throughout the Andes for centuries."

He looked around at each individual face that surrounded the campfire, making an intentional connection with each set of eyes.

"Pachamama, Mother Earth, has allowed us to enjoy the beauty of the Andes," Antonio said. "To give thanks, we pour out some chicha to honor her."

He tipped his drink and allowed a splash of chicha to fall from the cup. As it splashed on the ground, the rest of the trekkers did the same.

"For Pachamama," Antonio said.

Quinn nodded in appreciation; he felt a sense of understanding cultivating within him.

"Now," Antonio said, "let's eat!"

The meat was lightly seasoned with salt and pepper. It tasted like beef with an amplified toughness that Quinn hadn't experienced before.

"What is it?" Quinn whispered.

"It's alpaca," Antonio announced.

Quinn shrugged and took another bite. As he looked around the silent circle, he saw the trekkers scarfing their meals, hungry from the hike. But, as plates began to empty, Quinn felt a sense of awkwardness envelop the group.

"Since we're going to be hiking with each other for a while,"

Antonio said, "let's get to know each other a little bit."

A few people in the circle laughed.

"Let's go around and have everyone introduce themselves," Antonio said. "Name. Country. Occupation. And your reason for trekking to Machu Picchu."

Antonio looked to his left, which meant Quinn would be at the end of the circle. A man with tan skin and long, black hair set his plate down and began to speak.

"I'm Chris," the man said in Spanish. "I'm from Singapore. I'm in college, traveling through South America for the summer."

Quinn analyzed Chris. His style suggested that he was an authentic traveler, but his demeanor hinted toward privilege, a feature Quinn knew all too well.

Chris appeared connected to the past path that had brought him to the present moment. But there was something else about Chris that Quinn couldn't pinpoint. Like Chris knew something that Quinn didn't. Like Chris had been here before.

"When my parents flew me down here, I knew I had to go to Machu Picchu. I mean, I've been to Angkor Wat, the Pyramids of Giza, and the Great Wall of China. So, I just had to knock Machu Picchu off my list, too."

He smirked and looked around the circle, impressed with his own accomplishments.

Antonio smiled and looked toward the next trekker in the circle. The man set his plate on the ground, lifted his eyes, and smiled at the group.

"Hello," the man said in Spanish. "My name is Francis. I am from the West Coast of Africa. A country called the Ivory Coast."

Francis looked around the circle for glimpses of understanding. He saw a few heads nod in recognition.

Quinn noticed Francis's focus on the moment, on the present state of existence.

"I used to work as an accountant," Francis continued, "but I decided to take a break from the demands and the stresses of the job, opting to travel the world. I wanted to see what true freedom felt like. I wanted to experience the act of living in the present moment all the time."

I can't compete with that, Quinn thought.

"So, I traveled to South America and bought an old car," Francis continued. "I've driven through countries like Brazil, Argentina, and Chile gathering information that I can bring back to my own country. Here, at the end of my trip, I decided to trek to Machu Picchu to experience the majestic history of the legendary city."

Antonio nodded and thanked Francis for sharing his story. Looking at the woman next to Francis, Antonio opened his palm, inviting her to share her introduction. Averting her eyes, she wound her finger around her black hair.

"My name is Rosa," she said in airy Spanish. "I'm a journalist from Barcelona. I've lived in Argentina for a few years, covering the effects of climate change on South America, and the disorganized political divisions of Antarctica."

Antonio smiled, inviting her to continue.

"I decided to trek to Machu Picchu," Rosa said, "because I know it won't be here for much longer. I wanted to see it before an upcoming catastrophe destroys it."

Her eyes seemed to gaze into the future, perpetually thinking forward, aware of how one current step could impact the path ahead.

The circle fell into a still silence, interrupted only by the crackling of the fire. Finally, Antonio motioned for the next trekker to speak. Too focused on what he was going to say, Quinn tuned out as the next few members of the circle shared their stories.

As the trekker next to Quinn finished talking, Antonio motioned for Quinn to share with the group. His legs shook. Quinn tried to pretend that they shook from the impending chill. Or maybe from overuse on the day's hike.

Quinn wasn't afraid of public speaking at work. He gave presentations all the time. But those were about topics he knew well: money and numbers. He wasn't used to talking about himself.

"Uh, hey," Quinn said.

Deepening his voice, he felt an overwhelming sense to act sophisticated and young simultaneously, a certain pressure to act American, whatever that meant.

"I'm Quinn Thomas," he said. "I'm from the States. I used to work at a major firm. You know, corner office, a lot of responsibility."

He looked around the circle, trying to gauge his audience. Blank stares greeted him in return.

"But," Quinn continued, "I quit my job because I wasn't feeling fulfilled. And I booked a ticket to South America. Some guy told me that I needed to climb Machu Picchu while I was here. Maybe it'll help me find myself, or something."

With more blank stares coming from the circle, Quinn felt himself retreat. He was grateful for the dark sky; people in the circle couldn't see his face turn red.

Luckily, Antonio took control of the crowd.

"Thank you, Quinn," Antonio said. "Now that we all know each other a little better, let's wind down for the night. We have an early morning and long trek over Salkantay Pass tomorrow.

We'll wake up before sunrise. Be ready."

The trekkers stood and wandered to their tents, but Quinn remained seated on the stone. The fire smoldered.

Looking up, Quinn saw stars twinkling against a black sky, more stars than he had ever seen. And, looming below the constellations, stood the shadow of impending mountain peaks.

Chapter 9

Quinn sat alone. He placed another log on the campfire and listened to it crackle. His eyes followed a thin line of smoke that trailed upward toward the stars. As night thickened, more stars emerged.

Most of the other trekkers were either asleep, or in the process of getting ready for bed. Quinn clutched his new cup of hot coca tea, mostly for comfort against the mountain air.

Being alone felt unfamiliar to Quinn. Usually, he was surrounded by people in the office, or crowds walking to their next destination. Even cars and city noises made him feel accompanied. When he sat alone in his apartment in the city, he turned on the television, or looked at his phone to find some form of connection.

But here in the Andes, an overwhelming sense of loneliness devoured him. The pure darkness of the sky. The mountain atmosphere, void of artificial noise. The absence of crowds and convenient connection.

For the first time, Quinn sat alone with nothing but his own thoughts, his own fears.

He looked up at the sky again and traced the silhouette of the mountain ridge along the star-spotted black canvas. Nothing was above him except the night sky.

Time seemed to stop.

And then he heard the sound of vegetation crunch behind him in the dark.

"Hey, Quinn!" Chris shouted.

He appeared from the darkness, transforming from a shadow into a visible human as he stepped into the campfire's sphere of light.

"Mind if I join you?" Chris asked.

Quinn needed a break from the quiet, so he motioned for Chris to sit on a stone across the fire pit. As he sat, Chris almost seemed to flicker, as if, somehow, he was part of the smoke.

"Everyone else went to sleep," Chris said. "I'm still not used to the time difference between Peru and Singapore. I'm feeling pretty restless."

"Me too, I guess," Quinn said. "I'm not used to all this... quiet."

Chris laughed and jabbed the fire with a stick.

Unsettling silence crept into the circle. Quinn thought about Antonio's advice: connect with fellow trekkers.

Here we go, Quinn thought.

He took a deep breath and spoke, trying to sound casual.

"So," Quinn said, "you're from Singapore?"

Chris nodded. He ran his hand through his long hair before placing a knit cap on his head to ward off the chill.

"Singapore is a fun place," Chris said. "A very modern place, in fact. A lot like your American cities."

"Really?" Quinn said. "I assumed it was more of a village atmosphere."

Chris smiled, shaking his head at the misconception.

"That's what a lot of Westerners think when they envision any other part of the world," Chris said. "But we're just like

63

you."

"How so?" Quinn asked.

"Well, our economy is booming," Chris said. "We have a lot of rich people in Singapore. And that's the goal: get as rich as possible. Buy more things with your money, like a big house, or a fancy condo in a high-rise somewhere downtown. Sports car. Nice suits. Gold watches."

Chris eyed Quinn's intrigued expression.

"You know how it is," Chris said. "You're American."

Quinn dropped his head and glared at the embers beneath the campfire. A sense of guilt crept into his mind.

"My parents know what it was like before that attitude engulfed Singapore," Chris said. "My mom always talks about how much happier she was before all the high-rises and sports cars arrived."

"What do you mean?" Quinn asked.

"She said that people used to talk more," Chris said. "They used to be more creative, more fun. She used to focus on work that actually helped people live better lives instead of work that just earned her more money, more money that she could use to buy more stuff."

"But that's the point of work," Quinn said. "You work to earn money so you can buy things that make you happy."

Chris shrugged his shoulders and leaned forward, resting his elbows on his knees.

"That might be the point of work now," Chris said, "but it wasn't back then, before Western ideologies took over Singapore."

Quinn raised an eyebrow and crossed his arms.

"Before my country started to focus on working with the goal of making money," Chris said, "we used to work toward something that would help people and bring joy. Farming. Teaching. Fishing. People would work as long as they needed to, and then they would spend time just being with each other. Things were less busy. Less self-centered. More focused on others."

"But how were your parents so happy without any money, without any things to make them happy?" Quinn asked.

Chris lifted his eyes and looked at Quinn with conviction.

"Let me ask you something," Chris said. "Does your money make *you* happy?"

Quinn felt like he had been punched in the heart. The whole reason he had quit his job and left the United States for Peru was to escape the trappings of unhappiness, of discontent. But the concept of materialism was ingrained in his mind, in his habits, in his goals. He looked at the fire again and watched the flames shift.

"Honestly," Quinn said, "I thought it did. But since I've been here, I've started to realize that I don't know what makes me happy."

Chris nodded and snapped his fingers.

"I came to the same realization, *amigo*," Chris said. "My parents started from nothing and worked their way to the top of the food chain in Singapore. Now they have a penthouse in a skyscraper on the waterfront. I grew up with everything. Private school, the best clothes, cars, money, you name it."

"That's amazing," Quinn said. "Seriously impressive."

"Why is that impressive?" Chris asked.

Quinn fixated on a smoldering ember at the bottom of the fire.

"It's impressive because your family was able to rise from nothing and become successful," Quinn said.

"My family is the definition of Western success," Chris said.

"Money, power, and possession."

He paused and looked into the fire.

"But are we happy?" Chris said. "No, we are not."

He smiled one of those sad smiles that came from a place of past contemplation.

"So tell me," Chris said. "How is that successful?"

Quinn should have seen this message coming, but he felt blinded by his own definition of success, his own metric for what determined his self-worth. His own society had spoon-fed this message to him all his life. Commercials pushed him to want more things. Politicians fought for more money. Even his own family talked about other people's success solely in terms of their monetary value.

And for his entire life, Quinn had just accepted it.

"Should we put another log on the fire?" Quinn asked. "Or are you heading to bed?"

Quinn looked up at the stars and felt a sudden sense of loneliness again.

"I should probably go to bed," Chris said. "We're getting up early and we have a long day of hiking ahead of us."

"Good point," Quinn said.

Chris stood to leave, but Quinn remained seated on his rock.

"Hey, Quinn," Chris said. "Remember: you define your own success. Don't let society do that for you."

Quinn nodded. He waved awkwardly as Chris turned to leave the campfire. Quinn watched as Chris walked into the darkness, disappearing into the shadows of the mountain.

Something about Quinn's own past began to stir inside his soul. He couldn't name it, exactly, but he knew it was there.

His childhood had been idyllic. His parents had been support-ive. They had given him all of the things and opportunities that any American kid could ever want: a new bike on Christmas, traveling sports teams, vacations to tropical islands, a high-profile private middle school.

Yet, somehow, Quinn felt a yearning for more. A desire, deep in his core, that seemed insatiable. A thirst that felt unquenching.

Somewhere out there, Quinn knew that there was more to life, that happiness and contentment actually existed. And throughout his entire life, he had been told that this void could be filled with the pursuit of more.

But as Quinn moved further along this pursuit, he felt himself growing more and more discontented. Maybe a mindshift would do some good.

How did I get here? Quinn thought.

Lost in thought, Quinn watched the fire dwindle into low-burning coals. He poured water over the fire and stood to find his tent in the darkness.

Thinking about his own definition of success, Quinn crawled into his sleeping bag. He closed his eyes, still surprised at himself for making a spontaneous choice to sleep in the mountains of Peru. Eventually, the sound of the still mountains lulled him to sleep.

Chapter 10

Quinn opened his eyes and saw his own breath. As he reached his arm out of his sleeping bag, he felt the frigid morning air and dove his arm back into warmth. A faint light illuminated his tent, blanketing the interior in orange and eliminating the possibility of going back to sleep.

He heard voices near his tent, followed by footsteps that seemed to get closer.

"*Buenos días*, Quinn," Antonio said. "I have brought you coca tea."

Hesitantly, Quinn unzipped his sleeping bag. The rush of Andean air flooded his nerves with resistance, but he pushed himself up and unzipped his tent. Antonio crouched near the opening with a steaming mug. Antonio's chipper smile contrasted with Quinn's grouchy demeanor.

"Ready to summit Salkantay Pass this morning, *amigo*?" Antonio asked.

"Sure," Quinn grumbled, taking the mug from Antonio's hand.

Antonio nodded and eyed the mug.

"Coca tea," Antonio said. "It'll give you energy to push you over the mountain."

Quinn feigned a smile and drank.

"Breakfast is ready," Antonio said. "We start our climb in 15 minutes."

A sudden urgency filled Quinn's mind. As Antonio stood to leave, Quinn jumped out of his tent and threw on his clothes. He rolled his tent and packed his backpack, interspersing the process with sips of tea.

He placed his pack against a rock and walked to the campfire, where Antonio stood with his own mug of tea. Antonio motioned to a large container of purified water in the dirt. Quinn unscrewed his water bottle, lifted the water container, and filled his bottle. Placing his bottle in his backpack, Quinn finally made it to the minimal breakfast spread.

After spreading jam on a few slices of bread and stashing a granola bar in his pocket, Quinn sat on the same rock he had used as chair the night before. Unsure when Antonio would make the call for departure, Quinn scarfed his food. Slowly, the other trekkers wandered into the campfire circle with their prepared packs and food.

Quinn nodded to Francis, who pulled a bandana with the Ivory Coast's flag colors over his head. Rosa walked into the circle and recorded some rapid thoughts on her small audio recorder before sitting to eat. Chris wrapped his long hair into a bun and lifted his bread toward Quinn, smiling with jam-filled teeth.

After most trekkers had eaten, Antonio strolled into the circle. He stood without speaking; instead, he looked around at the jagged mountains, at the cloudless sky.

"Good morning, everyone," Antonio said.

His eyes remained fixed on the sky.

"Today, we will summit Salkantay Pass," he continued. "This journey will take us through the shadows of the sacred mountain: Salkantay."

Antonio pointed toward the mountain peak. Quinn followed Antonio's gaze. His eyes continued to lift until his attention settled on the 20,000-foot peak that towered above the entire Andean landscape.

"This mountain," Antonio continued, "is a revered mountain to Inca people. It provides life. It serves as a reminder of nature's power, of humanity's insignificance."

Lowering his gaze from the mountain, Antonio looked at the group of trekkers and smiled.

"The mountain pass will take us around that mountain," he continued. "We will surpass 15,000 feet."

He sipped his coca tea and watched as the trekkers's eyes popped.

"This will be the most physically demanding leg of our journey to Machu Picchu," Antonio said. "The slope is severe. The altitude is thin. Some of you might be tempted to stop, to give up, to turn around."

Antonio snuck a glance at Quinn, who lowered his attention in slight embarrassment.

"But," Antonio continued, "I guarantee that, when you summit the pass, you will understand the true meaning of success."

Quinn knew that Chris was looking at him, trying to catch his attention. But Quinn forced his eyes to focus on the mountains, too proud to admit that he recognized Chris's perspective.

"*Listos, amigos,*" Antonio said.

He threw his backpack over his shoulder and began walking toward Salkantay's peak. The trekkers looked at each other, hesitant to make the first step. The mountain towered, imposing.

Finally, Chris broke from the group and followed in Antonio's wake. Francis followed. Quinn did not want to feel left behind, so he stepped onto the single-track pathway and fell in line.

No one spoke. Quinn listened to the mountain wind as it struggled to overcome the Andean peaks that surrounded the wide, sparse valley in which little more than small flowers could survive. A bead of sweat dripped from Quinn's hair, but cooled in the high altitude. Reaching into his backpack's side pocket, Quinn grabbed his red bandana and tied it around his head to catch the growing stream of sweat.

The group had only walked a few hundred meters, but Quinn felt the effects of high altitude in his lungs. Or maybe it was a lack of physical fitness. Or both. Either way, the thought of stopping to rest was already piercing through his motivation. A near-vertical pathway rose before the group, but it remained far in the distance, taunting Quinn's energy, assuring him that the journey would only get more difficult.

Antonio stepped to the side of the line and encouraged Chris to lead the group. Catching Quinn, Antonio handed him a pouch of coca leaves.

"Chew a few of these," Antonio said. "They helped the Inca adjust to the altitude hundreds of years ago, and they continue to help the Andean people thrive up here."

Quinn nodded as Antonio bounded ahead of the group to reclaim his place at the front of the line. Pinching a few leaves between his fingers, Quinn placed them in his teeth and chewed. The familiar earthy flavor filled his mouth. As he chewed, the leaves retained their structure, not dissolving, which allowed him to chew the leaves like gum. Maybe it was the leaves's medicinal effect, or maybe it was a mind game, but Quinn felt his motivation increase as he strolled toward the peak.

Then, the trail began its incline. Quinn watched his feet, each step angling upward. The pathway around his boots grew rockier; the edges contained less grass as the path rose altitude. To compensate for the steep rise, the path zigzagged through a seemingly endless series of switchbacks.

It made little difference to Quinn. His lungs burned.

Each step took Quinn another foot in elevation. Each breath became more labored than the last.

Quinn reached for another pinch of coca leaves. As he chewed, he felt a wave of confidence swell within him. His breathing eased. More energy propelled him forward. And upward.

"Look how far we've already hiked," Antonio announced.

Glancing backward, Quinn saw the previous night's camp far below near the river in the open valley. He traced the trail from the camp to the base of the mountain. It looked like they were nearly halfway to Salkantay Pass.

A sense of pride swelled within him. He could not recall a time when he had overcome a physical challenge like this. Or a mental challenge, for that matter. Sure, he had pulled caffeine-induced all-nighters at the firm to finish a project on his own while his boss sat in the company suite at the basketball arena.

But this type of mental challenge was different. With every step, his mind told him to stop. And, with every step, Quinn told himself to keep moving. No amount of money or elaborate job title mattered. He had spent so much time in the past defining his success by the standards of other people, by the standards of materialism and greed. Now, the only thing Quinn cared about was making it to the top of the mountain pass. Not to please anyone else. Just himself.

Sweat cascaded from his forehead. His bandana, drenched, did little to stop the waterfall. And Quinn loved it, the physical manifestation of effort, of potential success. He paid no attention to anything else, to any*one* else. Rosa followed in Quinn's wake, but he paid no attention to what she thought. All he cared about was the next step up the path.

After a three-hour vertical journey, the winding path emerged into an open grassland. Rocks towered above the sparse plain. A few donkeys moved through the high altitude terrain, carrying gear for other groups. Quinn watched their slow, methodic temperaments.

I never thought I'd envy a donkey, Quinn thought, laughing to himself.

The group moved silently through the low grass in a single-file line, each caught in their own trance-like state. Eventually, the open field narrowed, funneling the line into another vertical, rock-covered pathway. Quinn felt his legs lose energy. He reached for another pinch of coca leaves.

Antonio moved up the path, his effortless pace encouraging Quinn to follow.

Each step drained Quinn's quads. Each rocky foot placement wobbled his ankles and calves. His pack weighed his back muscles down. He felt like one wrong step would send him tumbling back down the mountain, all the way to Cusco.

Then, Quinn took a horizontal step. The vertical path had ended.

Standing upright, Quinn looked forward and saw a panoramic view of the snow-capped Andes Mountains spanning in all directions.

"We made it," Antonio said. "Salkantay Pass."

He looked at each trekker, pausing to make purposeful connection with each person, cementing the gravity of the moment in their minds.

Quinn planted his feet on the rocky ground. Wind whipped around the sacred mountain and cooled the sweat on Quinn's bandana. He found a boulder and sat down, breathing heavily, gratefully, through the thin air.

His eyes caught Salkantay Peak. As he lifted his gaze upward, he saw a massive condor riding the wind.

Overwhelmed by the sense of success, of flight, Quinn began to cry

Chapter 11

Quinn wiped his tears with his bandana before anyone could see him, but the surreal feeling of accomplishment lingered.

The sun pierced through thin air and charred Quinn's face, countered by frigid mountain wind. He took a drink of water from his nearly empty bottle and placed it back in his pack.

Antonio stood near a cliff with his arms spread wide toward the panoramic landscape. He turned toward the trekking group and motioned for everyone to join him. As the group gathered, he removed a pouch of coca leaves from his pack and handed one to each hiker.

"We have made it to the top of the pass thanks to the grace of Pachamama, Mother Earth," Antonio said in Spanish. "It's time to show our gratitude."

He crunched the dried coca leaf in his hand, muttered something that resembled a prayer, and tossed the leaf dust into the mountain breeze. Stepping into the group, he motioned for another trekker to take his place.

For some reason, Quinn felt a pull to follow Antonio's ritual, to produce some outward form of joy for this new feeling of emotional freedom. He stepped forward near the cliff's edge and crushed the leaf in his hand. He pushed through the conditioned embarrassment that crept into his psyche and proclaimed his gratitude.

"Pachamama," Quinn said, "thank you for giving me the chance to overcome this mountain, to push through doubt, and to see this incredible view. Please stick with me along their journey and give me more opportunities to better myself, to change myself, to evolve."

Quinn lifted his arms and released the coca leaf dust into the breeze. He watched as it swirled through the current and dissipated into the mountain.

The trekkers looked at Quinn with wide eyes, unsure about the American's authenticity. But Quinn saw a spark in Chris's eye, a notion that acknowledged growth. As Quinn made room for the next person to show gratitude, Antonio smirked, proud of Quinn's progress.

After each trekker threw their leaves and spoke to Pachamama, Antonio announced a break for lunch. Quinn looked around for Chris, but he seemed to have disappeared. Most of the other trekkers had dispersed throughout the pass to eat in solitude. Quinn pulled a sandwich and a bar from his pack and found a solitary rock for a chair.

Staring at the panoramic view of the Andes, Quinn found a condor riding the wind. With his eyes, he followed the condor as it rose higher and higher. The silence absorbed Quinn's focus.

"What a view," Francis said.

Startled, Quinn kicked his feet out and almost dropped his sandwich.

Francis found a rock next to Quinn. He placed his pack on the ground and removed his food from the main pocket. He slid the Ivory Coast bandana from his head, revealing short, black hair, matted down by sweat.

"The Andes are beautiful," Quinn said. "I've never seen anything like this."

Francis nodded and took a bite from his apple. The sun moved behind a small cloud, sending a beam of light onto the mountain pass. For a moment, Quinn thought he saw Francis shimmer in the sunlight, like a prism.

"What other inspiring views have you seen in your travels?" Francis asked.

Quinn shook himself from the impossibility of physics and refocused on the question.

"To be honest," Quinn said, "I've never traveled outside of the States. Come to think of it, I actually haven't even traveled that much *within* the States."

"Really?" Francis said. "Why not?"

Quinn hesitated. He bit a chunk from his sandwich to stall for time while he planned his phrasing. Since landing in Peru, he had become aware of the American stereotype: insulated, ignorant, materialistic, and obnoxious. He did not want to fall into that role.

"My job never allowed me to travel much," Quinn said. "I worked at a pretty prestigious firm and, of course, that required me to spend a lot of time at the office. No time for a break when you're making money!"

Quinn shuddered at his own voice inflection. He knew that he had not escaped the stereotype. Francis's smirk erased any hope of that.

"All you Americans place so much value and self-worth on work," Francis said. "You all act like working long hours and making more money makes you a better person. Why is that?"

"I don't know," Quinn said. "I guess we just have this idea drilled into us from day one that, if we work hard, we can be successful, no matter our circumstances."

"And what determines your success?" Francis asked. "Money? The amount of possessions you can accumulate?"

Quinn looked at the place on his wrist where he usually wore a watch. He had a few watches. One with a black leather band and gold accents on the big face. One with a silver band and matching silver numerals. He even had a watch face that did not have numbers. And then, of course, there was the watch he wore for exercise. He rarely wore that one, unless it was his monthly trip to the gym.

A watch: a simple device used to tell time, to show the progression from the past to the future, second by second, minute by minute. But Quinn had always viewed a person's watch as something else: a sign of their success. A material representation of ambition and hard-work.

"Up until my conversation with Chris last night, I would have defined myself by my financial worth, by all the stuff that I had," Quinn said. "But now, I really don't know. I felt pretty successful trekking up that mountain pass."

Francis chuckled, steadying himself on the rock.

"How could you have felt successful if you didn't have all your money and materials with you?" Francis said.

Quinn dropped his head and laughed at the sarcasm.

"Alright, Francis," Quinn said. "How do you define *yourself*?"

"That's the most important question a person can ask themself," Francis said. "It's not easy to define ourselves honestly because we're always growing and evolving, always influenced by someone or something around us. But, the important thing is to continue that introspection."

He took a drink from his water bottle and looked out at the sprawling mountains.

"Let me tell you a story," Francis said. "In the Ivory Coast, where I'm from, I worked at a job that was very demanding. I loved it. At first I did, anyway. You see, I started my own accounting firm. I started out small, mostly doing taxes and helping small businesses with their bookkeeping. But then, a certain client walked through my door, and my life changed."

His eyes fixated on a condor that circled a valley in the distance.

"It was a client who sold products that most governments frowned upon," Francis continued. "I was not aware of their specific dealings at first. It was only until *after* they had paid me to keep their books that I understood the nature of their business. But, by then, it was too late. I was locked in."

As Francis took a bite of his apple, he looked at Quinn, reading his face for how the story was landing.

"They paid me handsomely to make their books and accounts look legal and still add up," Francis said. "And the nature of their business was nonstop, around-the-clock. I started spending more time at the office, and less time with my family. Sure, I provided money, but I was not providing my time and focus. I was not focused on the present joy that stood right in front of me. I dropped kindness as a priority. I became mean, getting upset at every little thing."

Quinn listened intently as the wind carried Francis's voice.

"I tried to buy back my wife's affection with gifts that I could afford from my job," Francis said. "But the gifts were empty. No kindness or honesty supported them. Eventually, she divorced me. Not even diamonds could keep her."

"Man," Quinn said, "I'm so sorry to hear that."

"Don't be," Francis said. "I did it to myself. And I learned a valuable lesson."

"What's that?" Quinn said.

"Always treat others with kindness," Francis said. "Especially those closest to you. They don't care about your money, your title, and they definitely don't care about the stuff you buy them. All they care about is how you make them feel."

Quinn wondered what his ex-girlfriend was doing in the city. She was probably at a nightclub with her friends, dancing the night away, living in the present moment without a care in the world.

"So," Quinn said, "what brought you to Peru?"

"My wife found out about the nature of my accounting business. She divorced me," Francis said. "She took my children and moved to another city to begin a new life, away from the potential threats of my work. It was the money that had corrupted me. I valued it too much. I knew I had to get rid of that influence."

Quinn leaned forward, inviting Francis to divulge more detail.

"I booked a one-way ticket to a place that was far from the organization's reach: South America," Francis said. "I bought a van and have been traveling the continent for over two years. Every city I stop in, I try to do good deeds for people. I try to use my power for the betterment of humanity every single day. I want to repay the kindness that I lost. A form of penance. Maybe someday I can earn my family back. And, if not my family, at least I can salvage my self-respect."

Quinn's eyes widened at the unexpected display of honesty. A tear dropped from Francis's eye, shimmering in the sunlight.

"That's incredible," Quinn said, attempting to break the silence. "Most people don't have the courage to make that move."

"Yes, but they should," Francis said. "I have become so much happier since ridding myself of my stuff, of my attachment to money, to greed. I no longer define myself by it either."

Quinn nodded and narrowed his eyes.

"Back to my original question," Quinn said. "How do you define yourself?"

Francis smirked.

"I define myself through my kind actions," Francis said. "Through my good works. And, most importantly, through simplicity: experience, knowledge, even breathing."

Francis smiled and shoved the remainder of his lunch into his backpack. Intaking the panoramic mountain view, he closed his eyes and breathed.

Chapter 12

As the morning sun crested the tallest mountain peak, the trekking crew began their journey down the steep slope of South America's Continental Divide. Despite his exhaustion from the climb to Salkantay Pass, each descending step sent more oxygen into Quinn's lungs.

They followed a single-file pathway that moved into a valley. The barren, rocky landscape transitioned into a highland climate: low shrubs and vast grass patches swept the vertical cliffs. Pools of clear snowmelt trickled along, fusing together to forge a small, winding stream that flowed parallel to the hiking path.

Antonio moved at a brisk pace, leading the group along the river's edge. Though reinvigorated after the break, Quinn trailed the line. His conversation with Francis lingered.

As he walked, he felt his breathing become less labored. For once, he noticed the change in the air, in the way it tasted. Crisp and refreshing, like a cool drink of water. With every few feet of descent, Quinn noticed the air become thicker, more humid, like the city, only without the aftertaste of exhaust and pollution.

He was noticing these things for the first time. And he appreciated it.

A loud sound echoed through the valley, starling Quinn from

his alignment with nature. His steps became cautious. His ears were curious, and his muscles twitched with attention.

As the group turned a corner, Quinn saw the source of the noise: a herd of cows roaming the 13,000-foot grasslands.

"They sound like dinosaurs," Antonio said, laughing as he looked back at the nervous group.

Francis and Chris sparked a conversation near the front of the line as they walked, likely sharing stories about their travels to faraway places. Quinn wanted to work his way up to the front of the line and join the conversation, but he hesitated and decided to remain in the back of the line.

He appreciated his discussion with both travelers, but they intimidated him. They were so worldly, so well-traveled. And they each possessed conviction in their beliefs, rooted in introspection and examinations of serious life experiences. Quinn knew he could never compete with that.

But maybe that was the problem. Maybe he did not *need* to compete. He had viewed life as a competition for so long, and that concept continued to hold firm. But life was not a competitive endeavor. Life was meant to be lived. And Quinn knew that if he continued to measure his own life against the experiences of other people, he would never win. Someone would always have more money, a better job title, a nicer car, a bigger house. Then again, did any of that stuff even matter?

It mattered to some people.

He thought about her.

Lucy.

Quinn had made the mistake of thinking that she loved him for *him*, not for his material worth. As soon as he told her about his decision to quit his job, she bailed. On to the next guy who could offer her more stuff.

He thought about Charlie, whose self-identified purpose in life was the pursuit of accumulation, of acquiring as much material wealth as possible, regardless of any human connection.

But there were other people out there who did not need material prosperity to feel successful, to feel worthy. There were people out there who valued kindness, experiences, simplicity, and helping others. And if that was who Quinn wanted to become, then he needed to find people who would walk that path with him. People like Chris and Francis.

"*Estamos aquí,*" Antonio shouted. "We've arrived at the Jungle Gate."

"The what?" Chris asked.

Antonio smiled as if he was waiting for someone to ask the question.

"The Jungle Gate is the entrance into the Amazon River Basin," Antonio said. "We might still be at 10,000 feet, but, from this point forward, we are no longer in a mountain climate."

Antonio made eye contact with each group member before continuing his explanation.

"From this point forward, you'll see the vegetation grow dense," he said. "The bugs will get bigger. The air will get thicker."

He paused to enhance the drama.

"From this point forward," he said, "you're in the Amazon Rainforest."

Quinn gripped his backpack straps as his adrenaline coursed. Antonio glanced in Quinn's direction. His look reminded Quinn why he had decided to take the adventure to Machu Picchu: to discover a real sense of life through new experience.

A simple, rocky outcrop defined the "Jungle Gate" as distinct, something intended to give pause to those who had walked this trail across centuries. It allowed travelers to appreciate the contrast in nature: mountain and valley; heat and cold; snow and vegetation.

For once in his life, Quinn felt present. *Actually* present. Not thinking about the next task, or his next response, or his next career move. He felt completely absorbed in the moment.

But his habits began to kick in. His mind wanted to drift toward the future, toward career goals and milestones that society had told him that he needed to achieve by a certain point in his life. The pressure to get married. That weighed heavily on his mind every time he closed his eyes. It seemed like every time Quinn talked to his parents, they asked him when he was going to pop the question, if he'd found a respectable girl to settle down with, when they were going to get some grandbabies. And everywhere he looked, society reinforced this message. Marketing material directed at him because of his age, presumably the age that most American men became fathers. Movies, where every guy that looked like him had settled down with a nice girl in a house in the suburbs. Quinn wasn't against this; in fact, he wanted to get married and start a family. But he despised the pressure. But he also gave into it.

And that's why he stuck with Lucy for so long, even though he knew she wasn't the one for him. Maybe that's why Quinn had decided to make her second place behind career advancement.

Or, maybe I am that self-absorbed and money-hungry, Quinn thought.

"Feel that humidity?" Francis asked, snapping Quinn from his thought circle.

"Yeah," Quinn said. "It's like it just appeared after we crossed the Jungle Gate."

Francis smirked and shoved Quinn on the shoulder.

"Look at you," Francis said, "noticing what surrounds you."

"I'm just trying to be like you," Quinn said. "Living in the present."

Francis laughed. He sped up his stride to get ahead of the group.

Quinn could feel a difference in humidity, but he couldn't decide why. Maybe it was the taste, a thick layer of water that filled his nose, or maybe the subtle weight of dense air that rested on his shoulders. Whatever the signals were, Quinn felt thrilled that he even noticed them at all.

With this focus on the present came a sense of simplicity. He was not wearing a designer suit or an ornate watch. He was not vying for attention from bosses or girls. He was not looking at a car upgrade or fantasizing about a more luxurious condo.

He was where he was. And he was content.

The group continued to move down the pathway. Francis pulled his bandana around his neck and forehead to ward off mosquitos. Quinn followed his example. Antonio pushed the pace in an attempt to reach the evening's destination before the temperatures rose too high for the unacclimated trekkers.

Winded and sweating, Quinn chewed on another bunch of coca leaves.

Eventually, the group moved onto a narrow dirt road. A few small wooden homes lined the road, hidden between jungle trees. Two kids kicked a soccer ball to each other. They paused when the trekkers came into view, but continued as soon as the group passed. A woman dressed in bright colors walked toward them. She nodded and smiled underneath her oversized hat brim.

Quinn marveled at the town's simplicity. It seemingly had nothing, yet it featured everything it needed, a stark contrast from his home city.

Shadows from the afternoon sun shaded the roadside vegetation as they moved out of the town's center. Pungent scents of fruits and soil wafted across Quinn's palette. And then he saw it: the coffee farm.

"We made it," Antonio said, pausing to wait for the trailing trekkers.

"Where?" Chris asked.

"Our home for the night," Antonio said. "Tonight, we'll sleep at this coffee farm. They're good friends of mine. They have space for us near the back of the farm."

The owner of the farm waved and greeted the group in Spanish, but spoke directly to Antonio in Quechua. She motioned for the trekkers to set up their tents toward the back of the property, which overlooked the jungle-covered mountains. Despite the heat and vegetation, they were still at 10,000 feet above sea level.

Quinn returned to the center of the farm to see a wooden table covered with food. As the rest of the group joined the table, Quinn ate to his heart's content. And then, the farmer called everyone toward a bush with red coffee beans. He seemed fully present. Something about his comfort level suggested that he had done this before.

"I want you each to take turns picking as many beans as you'd like," she said. "Then, peel the shell, like this. Place the beans in the pot and roast them over the fire."

She demonstrated the process with experienced dexterity.

"After that," she continued, " grind the beans here and make your coffee."

Quinn's eyes illuminated. He was a coffee fanatic, but he had never taken the time to understand how the magical concoction ended up in his disposable paper cups each day at the office.

As members of the group hesitated, Quinn stepped forward and picked a few dozen beans from the bush. He peeled the shells with difficulty, and then placed the beans inside the pot. As he stirred, he felt the heat from the fire. The color of the beans began to look familiar, so he removed them and threw the beans into the grinder. He poured boiling water over the beans and watched the liquid filter into his cup. The aroma invigorated him, a scent so familiar, yet so much more rewarding in its simplicity.

"You made your own cup of coffee from start to finish," Antonio said. "How does it taste?"

"It's the best coffee I've ever had," Quinn said.

Antonio smirked and returned his attention to Francis, who began to roast his coffee beans.

After hours of conversation and more coffee roasting, the sun began to set behind the mountains. The temperature dropped. The group began to dwindle. Quinn wandered toward his tent, but paused and sat in front of its entrance. His eyes traveled upward. He could hear the high jungle come alive. Unfamiliar sounds echoed through the leaves. A river rushed somewhere nearby. And the stars illuminated the night sky.

Chapter 13

The jungle was still dark when Quinn heard Antonio's boots outside of his tent. Curling into his sleeping bag, Quinn clutched to the last moment of warmth before he had to emerge into the elements.

"Coca tea," Antonio said through the tent fabric.

"*Si, por favor*," Quinn said. "*Un momento.*"

Taking a deep breath, Quinn removed his sleeping bag and put on a sweatshirt and beanie. He opened his tent and saw Antonio, crouched with a smile and a steaming mug.

"Good morning," Antonio said. "Are you ready for the most difficult day of our journey?"

Quinn stared at Antonio and blinked.

"You say that every morning," Quinn said.

"We're getting an early start today," Antonio said. "We have a lot of jungle to cover."

As Antonio moved on to the next tent, Quinn fell backward onto his sleeping bag. Two days of high altitude and miles of walking with a heavy backpack had taken its toll. His legs ached. His back hurt. His eyes wanted to close. He wanted to sleep, but he forced himself to sit up and pack. He was halfway to Machu Picchu, after all.

Quinn packed his tent and backpack before any of the other

trekkers. He stood alone in the center of the coffee farm's plaza. Although the sun would not crest over the mountains for another few hours, the sky had started to brighten, casting a dark blue hue across the nearly silent jungle.

The sound of boots startled Quinn from his thoughts. He turned to see Rosa emerge from the mist, a silhouette in the mystery of the Andes. She walked toward him. She smiled and held up one finger to Quinn as she spoke rapid Spanish into her audio recorder. When she finished, she moved closer to Quinn.

"Sorry about that," Rosa said. "I wanted to record my ideas before I lost them."

"No problem," Quinn said. "What are you recording for?"

"Since I'm a journalist for a newspaper in Spain," Rosa said, "I figured I would turn my trek to Machu Picchu into a story."

Quinn raised an eyebrow, impressed with Rosa's ambition. He noticed the camera attached to her backpack.

"I write about politics and the environment," Rosa continued. "And we've clearly been through some serious climate differences along our journey. Have you noticed the environmental impact that climate change has had on the Andes so far?"

Quinn blinked, unaware of any impact he had seen.

"It's okay if you haven't noticed it," Rosa said. "Most people don't. That's why my work is so important."

Work. Now that was something Quinn could relate to.

"You must get paid pretty well for your prestigious journalistic work," Quinn said.

Rosa furrowed her brow.

"I don't do it for the money," Rosa said. "I do it to help the future."

Antonio and a few other trekkers wandered over toward the center of the coffee farm, pausing the conversation.

Antonio grasped the straps on his backpack and breathed.

"Pachamama," Antonio said. "Isn't it beautiful? Such a different scene than yesterday morning."

Quinn looked around and noticed the dense jungle, a contrast to the alpine highlands that he saw yesterday.

"Our journey today," Antonio continued, "will lead us through the high jungles of the Amazon. It will be a long, hot day. Make sure to drink plenty of water."

He made eye contact with each member of the group.

"But it will be worth it," Antonio said. "Around sunset, we'll reach Aguas Calientes. The basecamp for Machu Picchu. And tomorrow morning, we'll finally see the legendary city."

Antonio nodded for emphasis. He turned and began walking along the path.

Rosa followed, and Quinn trailed behind her.

The entire group walked in silence for an hour, passing wild coffee and avocado plants. Occasionally, women dressed in bright colors with wide-brimmed hats walked along the path, causing Quinn to step aside. They passed wooden houses every half hour, each with its own small plot of farmland. But, for the most part, they passed through isolated, wild jungle that wound along steep mountain faces.

After an hour had passed, Antonio stopped and turned to face the group. He pointed toward a bright flower that hung from a tree.

"This flower is ayahuasca," Antonio said. "Medicine men brew it in tea and use it to induce dreams and visions."

He smirked.

"And white people come here from the States and use it," Antonio said. "It makes them go crazy."

Laughing, he turned and continued down the path.

Rosa looked back at Quinn and he caught her eye.

"You're not one of those people, are you?" Rosa asked, laughing.

"Definitely not," Quinn said.

"Well then," Rosa continued, "who are you?"

Quinn felt his breath quicken. He attributed the sudden pulse change to altitude and tried to ignore the anxiety that this question evoked. He wanted to appear successful and confident, an image he had cultivated throughout his entire life. That drive to maintain appearances had brought him to a wealthy firm in a big city. It had brought him an attractive girlfriend. On paper, he had achieved everything that his society told him that he needed.

Everything except happiness.

"The truth is," Quinn said, "I don't know who I am. I know who I *was*, but I don't know if I want to be that person anymore."

Rosa lifted an eyebrow, coaxing Quinn to continue.

"I guess that's why I came to Peru and decided to trek to Machu Picchu on a whim," he said. "To figure it all out."

Rosa smiled. The edges of her eyes creased. Her nose crinkled.

"Honesty," Rosa said. "I like that."

Quinn felt embarrassed, so he flipped the question.

"And who are you?" Quinn asked.

"As a journalist on foreign assignment," Rosa said, "I spend a lot of time alone. And I spend a lot of time thinking about that question."

Quinn stumbled on a rock, but caught himself and continued walking.

"I always wanted to tell stories," Rosa said. "And I always had a passion for standing up for a just cause. Writing and taking pictures allowed me to share those stories. So, I went to work for a newspaper in my home city: Barcelona."

"You're lucky," Quinn said. "Most people don't know what they want to do, so they settle for something until they figure it out. And most don't figure it out until it's too late."

"I suppose I am lucky in that sense," Rosa said.

She slowed her pace and allowed Quinn to catch up. A light rain began to fall. More of a mist in the air than a rain, enough to notice, but not enough for anyone to worry. As Quinn approached Rosa, though, he noticed her skin glimmer under the rain, almost translucent. His eyes focused, trying to decide if he was actually seeing what he thought he was seeing. And then, his foot caught an outgrown root.

"You alright?" Rosa asked.

Quinn felt his face flush.

"I'm fine, I'm fine," Quinn said. "Almost tripped, but we're good."

"Well, I'm glad," Rosa said. "We wouldn't want you to fall down the Andes Mountains."

She laughed, causing Quinn to chuckle at himself.

"So, what brought you to South America?" Quinn asked.

"My desire to stand up for a just cause," Rosa said.

She rolled her eyes and smirked at Quinn.

"I saw humanity striving for more," Rosa said. "More money, more materials, more fame. At the same time, I saw our world collapsing. Global warming, melting ice caps, drought, famine, disease. And I needed to tell that story."

The sun scorched Quinn's forehead, so he pulled his bandana lower to block the heat.

"Human greed has devastated most of the world already," Rosa said, "except for Antarctica. It has no natural resources that humans can exploit for profit; as a result, few humans live there, and no country or company owns it. Yet, I consider Antarctica to be the last frontier."

"Did you move to Antarctica?" Quinn asked.

"Argentina, actually," Rosa said. "I take regular journeys to Antarctica from there. But the real story isn't with Antarctica itself. It's with the countries that are positioning themselves to compete for Antarctica."

"But I thought you said Antarctica doesn't have anything that human greed would want," Quinn said.

Rosa turned her head toward Quinn and smiled.

"But it *will*," Rosa said. "Once someone discovers oil, or gold, or some metal that makes computer chips faster, there will be a mad dash for control of the continent. Just like there was for Asia, Africa, Australia, and the Americas."

"How do you know?" Quinn asked.

"I don't, and I hope I'm wrong," Rosa said. "But, if humans continue down this path of greed and materialism, control of Antarctica could cause another global war. The drive for more could end up destroying us all."

Quinn looked around at the dense jungle. Vibrant green leaves and tall trees shaded the shadowed path, interspersed by open patches of intense sunlight. The concept of this jungle turning into a wasteland seemed simultaneously impossible and likely. He felt each step grow heavier.

"Based on your research, how do we stop that from happening?" Quinn asked. "How do we get our world back from the brink of destruction?"

Rosa reached out and brushed a broadleaf with her hand.

"People don't care about anything other than what's right in front of them," Rosa said. "If we can get people to expand their idea of what actually impacts them, maybe we'll see a change."

"How do we get there?" Quinn asked.

"It all starts with the individual striving for happiness instead of materials, with caring about the collective longterm good instead of the momentary success or pleasure," Rosa said. "One person's mindshift can inspire others to do the same. Eventually, companies that produce a mass amount of stuff will see lost profits. Governments will campaign toward people's happiness instead of people's wallets. Then, maybe our society will see a change in priority. Then, we might see some hope for the future of humanity."

Rosa's smile faded into a look of defeat. She stepped to the side of the path and took a drink from her water bottle. She motioned for Quinn to continue moving forward. Quinn kept walking, following Antonio's footsteps across the jagged jungle path.

As he turned the corner, a suspension bridge appeared over a large canyon. The bridge's frayed rope and warped wood sent panic through Quinn's nerves.

"Alright, team," Antonio said. "Who is afraid of heights?"

Chapter 14

The bridge grew more imposing as Quinn neared the canyon. Peering through thick jungle, Quinn approached the canyon's ledge, where the vegetation thinned. Loose rock slid underneath his boots and sent a spike of fear through his spine. Quinn heard the echoes of river rapids far below the canyon's dropoff. He wanted to look down, but his self-preservation instinct forced him to cement his feet.

He looked at the long suspension bridge that swung in the wind over the canyon and tried to convince himself that the wooden planks were secure enough. But the reality of the situation clung to his thoughts.

"We're almost to our final stretch of the trek to Machu Picchu," Antonio said in Spanish. "All we need to do is cross this bridge."

He looked at Quinn and raised an eyebrow, daring him to face his fear.

"The bridge is safe," Antonio said, "but it can only support one person at a time."

The trekkers looked around at each other and began to murmur.

"I'll go first to show you it's safe," Antonio said. "Then, you decide who is brave enough to go next."

Antonio grasped the frayed rope and stepped onto the first wooden plank. As he moved toward the center of the bridge, it swayed and groaned. The trekkers stood in silence, awaiting catastrophe.

But it did not occur. Antonio stepped onto solid ground across the canyon and turned to wave the next trekker across the bridge. The trekkers stood still, locked in fear. No one made eye contact with another person, knowing that guilt from fear might override their common sense.

And then Quinn moved.

He stepped toward the entrance to the bridge with something that resembled resolve.

Grasping the rope handles, he set his foot on the wooden plank. He felt the bridge wobble beneath his weight, swaying his momentum from left to right. Pushing the thought of retreat from his mind, he stepped forward on the next plank. He took another step, and then another, all while keeping his focus forward, reminding himself not to look down.

As he moved toward the center of the bridge, he looked sideways and gazed at the vastness of the canyon. Glancing forward, he saw Antonio waving him forward. But, before taking another step, Quinn looked down. Through the spaces between the wooden planks, his nerves plummeted through the gaps, falling hundreds of feet toward the rushing river below.

He froze. His mind raced.

Questioning his decision to step onto the bridge, Quinn found his mind weaving through every decision he had made in the last month. He quit his secure, well-paying job at the firm. He broke up with his beautiful girlfriend. He flew to a foreign country with no plan. He embarked on a journey through a strange mountain range to find some mythical lost city. And now, he was stuck on a bridge hanging over a canyon in the jungle.

He knew that he was going to die.

Then, as Quinn swayed on the suspension bridge, he thought about Charlie.

What did his death mean? Quinn thought.

A sudden presence filled Quinn with fear. Yet, somehow, he felt more courageous. Quinn's life choices filtered through his mind. He had stacked up accomplishments from elementary school to his career. In the business world, his accolades had garnered him attention and a path forward, but they meant nothing in the middle of the Peruvian jungle. His ambition, solely focused on material accumulation, only weighed him down on the bridge. None of his material possessions, mone- tary accumulation, or business maneuvers had given him the courage to walk across this bridge. And that was the only goal that mattered: finding the courage to move forward toward meaningful success.

Antonio's shout snapped Quinn from his thought spiral.

"You're halfway there, Quinn!" Antonio shouted. "Keep going. Reach inside your heart and find the courage to fight the fear!"

Clutching the rope handle, Quinn forced his left leg to move. As he planted his foot on the wooden plank, he forced his right leg to follow. And then his left.

Eventually, his foot landed on solid ground. Antonio shook Quinn's hand, and then waved the next trekker across the bridge. Quinn stumbled toward a log and sat. He took a drink from his water bottle and watched Rosa cross the bridge with cautious courage.

While watching someone else cross the bridge after he had already completed the journey, Quinn realized that the path forward was not difficult. When he was on the bridge, his focus narrowed to each step without seeing the large picture. Now, away from self-centered focus and a perspective on the past, he understood. The bridge was not inherently fear-inducing; he walked in the same manner as he did on the ancient Andean pathway, or the city sidewalk. It was Quinn who had caused his own fear. He created his own difficulty.

Quinn wanted to approach his own future that way. He did not want to look back on his life and realize that there were obvious ways to enhance his own happiness, to discover his own purpose. He did not want to look back on his life and see that his own ego and self-absorbed mindset caused him to be miserable in the pursuit of material goods, in the pursuit of society's definition of success.

Rosa crossed the bridge and smiled at Quinn. Francis seemed to enjoy the bridge's sway, pausing every few steps to look down at the canyon. Chris followed. He looked back once to make sure the bridge would not collapse under someone else's weight.

Once all of the trekkers stood on the other side of the canyon, Antonio waved the group forward. They walked down a gravel road that led to a railroad track.

"We'll follow this track all the way to Aguas Calientes," Antonio said.

He pointed down the railroad, which seemed to disappear into the jungle.

"The walk will take about three hours," Antonio continued. "And be careful. This is an active track. Trains speed by every half hour. Don't get in the way."

Quinn followed Antonio down the track. The crossties provided a smooth stepping platform against the uneven gravel, but they forced Quinn to lengthen his stride. He decided to jump onto the iron track and balance for a while.

Dense jungle plants hung over the railroad, creating a tunnel. A river rushed nearby, somewhere through the vegetation.

Quinn thought about Rosa's investigative reporting. He could not fathom the idea of this jungle disappearing from climate change. And it would be directly caused by human greed, a greed that he had taken part in throughout his entire life, a greed that he had been bred to perpetuate.

He looked down the iron railroad and watched it pierce through the jungle.

Quinn no longer wanted to be a part of that future. He did not want to contribute to humanity's self-inflicted destruction. That lifestyle was not making him happy anyway. Material ambition was all he understood. He knew that he wanted no part of that greedy impulse any longer.

But he did not know what to do instead.

Chapter 15

The railroad track began to rattle. Loud thrashing echoed behind Quinn. He turned and saw smoke burst through the trees. He jumped over the iron railroad line and slid down the gravel hill, flatting himself against the jungle wall.

The train flew by, blowing hot air across Quinn's face. Blue and yellow paint blurred together in forward motion.

And then, the jungle was silent.

"These trains scare me," Francis said.

"They scare me too," Quinn said. "They're so close. If I reach out my hand, the train would snap it off."

Francis laughed and jumped back onto the railroad track.

"We should have another half hour before the next one comes," Antonio said.

Each train brought a short wave of conversation between the trekkers, but the endless path through the jungle seemed to invite silence. Quinn pushed forward. He had lost track of time. Aguas Calientes seemed close, but he was afraid to ask exactly how close. He did not want to hear that they still had two hours to go.

As Quinn fell into silent, monotonous walking again, he looked through the jungle tunnel and returned his thoughts to his own life's path. Until his trip to Peru, his life felt as monotonous as the railroad. Prescribed. Unadventurous. Without a meaningful purpose.

"Hey Quinn!" Rosa shouted, breaking the silence.

Quinn felt his pulse quicken as he turned to look.

"Do you have a *sol* coin?" Rosa asked.

Quinn reached into his pocket and pulled out a small coin.

"Next time a train comes by, put the coin on the track," Rosa said.

"Sounds dangerous," Quinn said. "And besides, that's a waste of money."

Rosa shook her head and laughed.

Soon, the rumbling of an oncoming train disrupted the stillness of the jungle. Flicking the coin between both hands, Quinn avoided eye contact with Rosa. He did not want to move toward the track when a train was charging in his direction.

"Do it, Quinn!" Rosa shouted.

Quinn turned and watched as Rosa placed a coin on the metal rail. She jumped away from the track and scampered to the edge of the jungle.

The train moved closer. Thick steam bellowed. The conductor blared the horn, imploring hikers to move away from the unstoppable force.

Stepping away from the train track, Quinn caught Rosa's eye. Her look showed disappointment. And Quinn could not handle it.

He sprinted forward, watching the train increase its speed. Quinn reached down and placed the coin on the rail. As he bounded backward toward the jungle, he felt the wind from the train rush by his face. Shaking, he stood by Rosa. She looked at him and laughed. Quinn felt his spine turn rigid as Rosa grabbed his hand.

And somehow, in the middle of the chaos, Quinn felt an overwhelming sense of comfort.

The train's blue-and-yellow blur sped away, leaving the jungle still again. Rosa pulled Quinn toward the train track. Letting go of his hand, Rosa began to dig into the rubble that lined the rail. Screaming with excitement, she pulled her *sol* coin from the ground and held it in the air. The sun reflected off the flattened, oval-shaped gold coin.

"Crushed by the train, but still here," Rosa said. "Still fighting for glory and splendor."

Quinn smirked as he knelt by the track. He saw his golden *sol* coin resting on the rail, right where he had placed it. The coin's impressions had stretched, crushed under the momentum of the train. Yet it still retained its beauty.

The coin felt hot in Quinn's hand as he peeled it from the rail. He put the coin in his pocket and continued the walk in silence along the train track.

The endless walk along railroad tracks lulled Quinn into monotony. He was familiar with monotony, the day-to-day grind that brought a perpetual dullness to life. But the railroad track's path was different. This monotony provoked a sense of calm, inducing a meditative state. And, in the front of his mind, Quinn knew that there was a final destination.

As he zoned his focus through the railroad track's tunnel of trees, he saw that final destination: Aguas Calientes. The railroad track bent somewhere in the distance, and buildings began to appear as the trees thinned.

The vegetation grew more sparse along the river's edge. Quinn saw tall, jagged peaks rise above the jungle. These monoliths seemed to shoot directly upward, sprouting from the river. A thin layer of clouds clung to the tops of the peaks, draping the mountains in mystery.

"A few more minutes and we'll be at our final stop," Antonio shouted.

Rosa looked back at Quinn and smiled.

"I can't believe we'll be at the base of Machu Picchu so soon," Rosa said.

Quinn smiled, but his eyes wandered above the towering mountains that lined the river. Thousands of feet above his head, covered in jungle, hid the ruins of an ancient fortress.

Chapter 16

The pillow enveloped Quinn as he dove on the bed. A real bed with a mattress and a comforter, surrounded by four walls and a roof. It seemed like an eternity since Quinn had sprawled within the trappings of modern comfort.

He bolted upright at the thought.

After camping outside in the open air surrounded by nature and simplicity, Quinn wasn't certain if he wanted to fall back into his old ways of modernity and comfort, of material possession. The amount of mental and emotional growth he had experienced in the last four days had transformed him more than the last four years.

He looked at his backpack, which sat discarded in the corner of the small hotel room.

Lifting himself from the sunken mattress, Quinn showered, cleansing days worth of dirt and sweat. After putting on relatively clean clothes, he left the hotel and emerged onto the main street of Aguas Calientes.

The town had a few side alleyways, but it mostly consisted of the main road that ran along the river. The town seemed to function solely as a basecamp for Machu Picchu enthusiasts.

Quinn strolled through a small market full of brightly colored trinkets and gifts, mostly themed after Machu Picchu. His legs felt light without the weight of his backpack, but the Andes had taken a physical toll, leaving his muscles shaky. As it neared dinner time, his stomach growled, so he decided to leave the market and find a place to eat. He saw a restaurant perched on a hill overlooking the river, so he climbed the stairs and sat at an empty table.

As soon as he had sat down, Antonio entered the restaurant. Catching Quinn's eye, Antonio waved and walked toward the table.

"Mind if I sit?" Antonio asked.

Quinn shook his head and motioned for Antonio to take the seat across the table. Antonio raised his hand and the server approached.

"*Dos cervezas, por favor,*" Antonio said. "*Cuando puedas.*"

The server smiled and moved to the bar. Antonio and Quinn sat in comfortable silence until the server returned with two beers.

"Cheers, *amigo,*" Antonio said.

The pint glasses chimed.

"Just think," Antonio said, "tomorrow morning, you'll climb up that mountain to see the legendary city of Machu Picchu. And then your journey will be over."

Antonio looked at Quinn and tried to gauge his inner thoughts, but Quinn suspected that he already knew them somehow.

"How do you feel about that?" Antonio asked.

Quinn's eyes followed the trees, up the side of the mountain, and into the clouds that hid the ancient city.

"To tell you the truth," Quinn said, "I don't know. I have conflicting emotions about the whole thing."

Quinn halfway hoped that he could end the conversation without further explanation, but Antonio's silent stare forced him to continue.

"Of course, I'm excited to complete the journey and see the ruins of Machu Picchu," Quinn said. "That was the whole point of the trek. It's what comes after the trek that I'm worried about."

"How so?" Antonio asked.

"Physically, this trek was the most difficult thing I've ever done," Quinn said. "I found so much joy and purpose through the simple act of walking through nature. I'm afraid that, when I return to the States, I won't be able to find that same sense of happiness that I came here to find. I don't want to feel…"

"Lost?" Antonio said.

Quinn nodded and took a drink and watched people walk by the restaurant along the main road. These people looked so happy, so fulfilled. Quinn had grasped fulfillment, but he recognized that it would slip away if he returned to his life as it was before, if he returned to the status quo of his own society's attitude.

Antonio saw the worry in Quinn's eyes.

"Let me tell you a story," Antonio said.

Quinn returned his glance to the table.

"In 1911, a Yale professor named Hiram Bingham came to Peru, searching for something that was lost," Antonio said. "He wanted to find the legendary lost city of the Inca, knowing that this discovery would bring him fame and glory."

He took a drink of his beer and continued.

"Bingham spent weeks trekking through the jungles of the Andes Mountains, unsure about where he was going or what exactly he was looking for," Antonio said. "He talked with people who lived around here. They told him about an old city on top of that hill up there."

Antonio nodded in the direction of Machu Picchu, invisible

from the road below the mountain.

"When Bingham and his team climbed the mountain and saw the ruins of Machu Picchu," Antonio said, "he believed that he had found the lost city of the Inca. He took pictures, wrote articles, and published his findings to the world. He became one of the most famous explorers of his lifetime."

"That makes sense," Quinn said. "Discovering a lost city in the jungle would boost an explorer's fame and fortune."

Antonio smiled. Quinn suspected that Antonio wanted him to say that.

"And that's where you're wrong, my friend," Antonio said. "You see, Machu Picchu was never lost. Andean people had been living in and around it for five hundred years."

His smile transformed into a smirk.

"It was not the city that was lost," Antonio said. "It was the explorer."

"What do you mean?" Quinn asked.

"Machu Picchu was never lost," Antonio said. "It knew where it was the whole time. Hiram Bingham did not. He was lost, discontented with his position in life. He needed to find the city in order to find himself. Not the other way around."

Antonio took a final drink of his beer and stood. Nodding to Quinn, he turned and left the restaurant.

The server appeared and placed a plate of meat and vegetables on the table. Quinn ate quickly, paid, and walked onto the main road by the river. The sun had dipped behind the mountains, casting dark shadows across the town. Walking underneath the streetlights, Quinn made his way back to his hotel. When he opened his door, he flopped onto his bed. He wanted to sleep; tomorrow's wake-up call was early. But, for some reason, he couldn't turn his mind off. The last few days swirled across his thoughts.

He thought about Chris, and his realization that acquiring more things did not bring him happiness in the past. He thought about Francis, and his discovery that identity comes through present actions, not materials. And then he thought about Rosa, and her warning about changing the way in which we live in order to secure a happier future.

As Quinn envisioned Hiram Bingham lost in the jungle, his mind drifted into sleep.

Chapter 17

The knock on the door shook Quinn from deep sleep. Coursing with adrenaline, he jolted upright and scanned the room. All dark, except for the faint light from the bedside alarm clock. 3:02.

Quinn heard voices. Calm voices. They spoke in rapid Spanish.

As his brain focused, he realized that the voices were coming from the alarm clock.

Someone knocked on the door again.

"Quinn!" Chris shouted from outside the door. "You awake?"

Quinn rubbed his eyes and sat on the edge of the bed.

"Yeah," he grumbled.

"Good," Chris said. "Open up. It's almost time to make the final climb."

Throwing a shirt over his head, Quinn stepped toward the door. The wood floor felt cold beneath his bare feet. His legs ached from days and miles through the Andes.

As he unbolted the door, Chris popped through. With a bandana around his long hair, Chris carried his backpack and excitement.

"You ready to explore Machu Picchu?" Chris asked.

"Your smile is way too chipper for this early in the morning," Quinn said. "Or this late at night. I can't tell."

"That's the spirit," Chris said.

Quinn brushed his teeth and put on his hiking clothes. His socks had dried, but they stunk. He put them on and laced up his boots. Chris sat in a chair in the corner of the room. His foot tapped. Something about him seemed to glow.

"Think about the journey that led us here," Chris said, too nervous to sit quietly. "We flew to a new country, joined up in Cusco, trekked up to a 15,000-foot mountain pass, emerged into the Amazon, slept at a coffee farm, and followed a railroad track to end up here: the base of the lost Incan city."

Quinn's excitement began to overtake his sleep deprivation, but he masked it with a stoic expression. He knew the journey was far from over.

"Ready," Quinn said.

He threw his backpack over his shoulders and walked into the narrow hallway. Chris followed. Quinn's backpack dragged against the walls of the staircase as he rounded the tight corners. After three sets of stairs, they stepped into the hotel lobby.

Francis sat on a couch. He looked up from the newspaper when he heard footsteps in the otherwise silent hotel.

"Hey, friends!" Francis shouted. "You ready for the big moment?"

"Of course we are," Chris said. "It has been a big lead-up."

"And the present moment is what it's all about," Francis said.

He slapped Quinn on the shoulder and pushed him out the door. The three trekkers walked along the main road until they came to the meeting point underneath the streetlight. Its orange glow pierced the darkness of Aguas Calientes.

"*Hola, chicos*," a voice said from the shadows.

Rosa's face illuminated as she moved closer to the light. She stood by Quinn and nodded to Chris and Francis.

"Well, guys," she said, "are you prepared for what Machu Picchu will bring?"

"What do you mean?" Chris asked.

Rosa smirked.

"Machu Picchu has been around for a long time," Rosa said. "It's story is legend. How will you respond to it when the time comes?"

Quinn stood in silence, unsure about what the future would bring. As they contemplated the gravity of the journey ahead, other trekkers filled in the circle. Then, a figure appeared in the shadows. As it moved closer, Quinn felt strangely calmer.

"*Amigos*," Antonio said, "the day is here."

Antonio emerged into the orange glow of the streetlight.

"I'll lead you across the bridge to the stone staircase," Antonio said. "We will climb upward for a few hours in total darkness. This might be the most difficult section of your journey, but know that the reward is on the other side."

Quinn laughed at Antonio's flare for the dramatic. His legs shook with fatigue at the thought of climbing stairs.

"As we near the top of the staircase," Antonio continued, "the sun will begin to light up the sky, just enough for you to see your steps. We will be the first people to enter Machu Picchu today. And we should see the sunrise above the sacred city. Just in time to see the magic of Machu Picchu."

With that, Antonio turned and walked into the shadows, disappearing like a phantom into supernatural fog. Mysterious fear crept up Quinn's spine, but intrigue pushed the fear from controlling his mind. With a deep breath, Quinn followed Antonio into the darkness. The other trekkers followed in silence; their footsteps echoed off the dark cobblestone street. Steep canyon walls rose up on both sides of Aguas Calientes and, though Quinn couldn't see them, he could feel their impending presence. The sound of the rushing river bounced off the canyon walls, the same river that had carved the canyon over the course of millennia, a far-reaching memento to the impact of time, the influence of the past upon the present.

The street was dotted with the orange glow of sparse street-lights. But after reaching the edge of town, the streetlights stopped, plunging the entire walk into darkness. Quinn walked in silence. He knew that the other trekkers followed behind him, but they seemed distant, unimportant as he drifted into thought. A calm overcame his nerves as he allowed himself to absorb into the darkness, into the mystery of Machu Picchu's final approach.

And then Antonio stopped. Quinn snapped from his medita-tive walk to see a bridge guarded by military-style patrols.

"*Pasaportes*," Antonio said to the trekkers.

Quinn scrambled to pull his passport from his backpack. He handed it to Antonio along with Rosa.

The guard checked each passport carefully against her entry list. As she handed each trekker their passports, she waved them across the bridge. Quinn followed the shadowed path until it reached a vertical stop.

"We've come to the final piece of your journey," Antonio said. "The Inca Staircase."

Quinn looked up and saw an intensely sloping staircase woven between the jungle that clung to the mountain's face.

"I'll follow the group up the route," Antonio said. "Stay true to the path and trust that you'll reach the end."

He nodded at Quinn.

"Headlamps on," Antonio said.

Quinn stretched the headlamp across his forehead and flipped on the light. Taking a calming breath, he stepped forward onto the first stone step.

The step rose higher than he anticipated. Quinn's foot caught on the step and he stumbled, but caught himself on the next vertical step. Rubbing his scuffed hand, he continued up the staircase. The headlamp provided some decent light, but it only focused on the stair ahead. The surrounding jungle remained clouded in darkness. As the trekking group weaved up the mountain, Quinn heard birds rustling somewhere nearby, chirping a warning song to neighbors. Heavier movement in the trees suggested larger animals. Quinn pushed the idea from his mind.

But other thoughts took its place.

His ex-girlfriend. Beautiful, vibrant, enlivening. And Quinn had dropped her. For what? To fly to a foreign country. To take a glorified nature walk. To be eaten alive by mosquitos and drink gritty tea from plants that would get him arrested in the States.

His old job. Profit, stability, status. But Quinn had quit his job on a whim because he felt some fleeting form of social awakening, some youthful desire to seek truth and happiness like he was some sort of religious figure instead of an average American.

His past life. His *real* life, the life he would return to at some point after this journey ended. Quinn's attempts at escape remained temporary, ineffective. Running to Peru only served the purpose of prolonging whatever uncertainty he felt about his old way of existing. What would he do when he returned? Would any of this even matter anymore?

His friend. Charlie Jacobson. Dead. Dead and incomplete. Dead and unfulfilled. Dead, yet, somehow, he still carried influence over Quinn through his death.

The carabiner that clung to Quinn's metal water bottle chimed, echoing the sound of chains through the still jungle.

Quinn peered through the darkness and found the next step, pushing his body upward toward the next one. His leg muscles shook. They felt drained, depleted of energy. But he knew the final goal stood high above, just out of reach.

The other trekkers had faded from his view, immersed in the darkness somewhere behind him. Jungle sounds and the echo of his own breath filled Quinn's ears. Sweat poured from his hair, drenching his shirt and bandana. His mind focused on each step. His attention zoned on the fine-tuned legs muscles that propelled him upward.

Finally, after more than an hour, the staircase flattened. Antonio waved in the twilight near the entrance to the ruins, which remained hidden from view. Quinn walked toward him, along with the other trekkers. Antonio's light guided them to the gate. Stepping aside, Antonio motioned for them to enter the city.

Quinn stepped through the gate and walked onto a platform that overlooked the ruins. The sun had just risen over the mountain peaks, casting a beam of light on the ancient buildings.

Tears fell from Quinn's eyes.

Chapter 18

The ancient city loomed in stillness as the sun pierced the mist. Quinn overlooked the silent, surreal scene. Nobody walked among the stone ruins.

From the platform, Quinn's eyes traced the descending grass that fell into a small concave on top of the mountain. The ruins sat compacted, yet clearly functional. A plaza in the middle of the city gave way to a steep incline, rising to the peak of Huayna Picchu. Through the fog, Quinn saw ruins on top of the peak.

"Think about everything that used to be here," Chris said.

Quinn turned and nodded, only halfway focused. Chris grabbed Quinn's backpack and shook it, indicating a successful mission.

Heavy footsteps stomped the grass behind him.

"I can't believe we're here," Francis said. "We're actually standing in Machu Picchu."

He stood by Chris, lining up to see the view.

"I wonder how we'll be transformed by this experience," Rosa said, appearing in line with the group.

Antonio stood next to Quinn and smiled.

"Alright, everyone," Antonio said. "We've made it to our goal: Machu Picchu. Now, go explore!"

Rosa, Francis, and Chris walked in different directions, evaporating into the fogged city. But Quinn's feet remained rooted to the platform. Antonio stood next to Quinn and stared into the expanse of history. Minutes of silence passed.

"This is the same view that Hiram Bingham saw when he first set eyes on the city," Antonio said. "The same view that reminded him that he was not lost."

"When he discovered Machu Picchu?" Quinn asked.

Antonio smirked.

"Bingham did not discover Machu Picchu," Antonio said. "Remember, it was always here, used and admired by the descendants of the Inca people."

Quinn glanced sideways at Antonio.

"Machu Picchu was lost to Bingham," Antonio said. "But the thing he was searching for was always there."

Fog began to lift from the ruins. A beam of sunlight illuminated the iconic mountain, silhouetting the city.

"Just as Machu Picchu was not truly lost," Antonio said, "neither are you, Quinn Thomas."

Quinn's eyes began to well with tears. An overwhelming sensation of inspiration overtook his locked emotional vulnerability. Dropping to his knees, Quinn began to weep. The mountains blurred. Flickers of sun rays flashed bulbs of light across Quinn's clouded eyesight, forcing him to wipe his tears away.

As he stood, Antonio gripped his shoulder.

"Though you will leave Machu Picchu," Antonio said, "Machu Picchu will never leave you."

Quinn eyed Antonio with suspicion.

"Do you know what today is?" Antonio asked.

Quinn shook his head.

"Today is *Inti Raymi*, the celebration of the Winter Solstice,"

Antonio said. "This celebration was banned by Catholic mission-aries and Spanish colonial rulers. But the Andean people con-tinued to celebrate in opposition. They continued to commune with their ancestors. They continued to ask their ancestors for help."

Antonio nodded toward Quinn.

"You, my friend," Antonio said, "have the honor of being in a sacred place on a sacred day. Do not waste this opportunity."

"What do you mean? Quinn asked.

"Recall the lessons you've learned along the trail," Antonio said.

Quinn thought about his conversation with Chris during their first night on the trek. Salkantay Peak loomed above the basecamp. Humantay Lake rested nearby. Quinn stood alone by the campfire, lost in thought and despair, until Chris appeared from the dense darkness that surrounded the campfire. Discussing his past and his family's history in Singapore, Chris revealed the decay that came with the desire for more things, more possessions to call one's own.

Quinn remembered the feeling of accomplishment that came with climbing Salkantay Pass. The condor swirled overhead as Francis sat and shared his story. He told Quinn about his escape from the materialistic idols of the Ivory Coast and his quest to find a simpler way to live.

Then, Quinn reflected on his journey through the dense jungle, the entrance to the Amazon. He recalled walking through thick fog; the jungle was shrouded in mystery as he walked with Rosa. Her research warned that, if humanity continued down its path of material acquisition and greed, impending devastation was imminent.

"Fueled by the past, we must live in the present to change our future," Antonio said. "You, Quinn Thomas, have the power to change your future."

Standing tall, Quinn felt his feet root themselves to the earth beneath his feet. A sudden connection to Machu Picchu filled his senses. He felt at peace, truly calm for maybe the first time in his life.

The sun rose higher, nearly above the mountains. A sun beam pierced the sky, warming the fog that covered the city. Almost instantly, the fog disappeared, revealing Machu Picchu's historical glory, cleansing fog away from the beautiful ruins.

Quinn turned to look for Antonio, but somehow, he was gone. Looking around in a circle, Quinn lost all sight of his guide.

"*Gracias*," Quinn whispered.

Stepping forward off the platform, Quinn took his first steps into Machu Picchu.

Chapter 19

The stone steps felt timeworn, beckoning Quinn back to a time long since forgotten. Each stride took Quinn closer to Machu Picchu's central plaza, surrounded by expertly crafted buildings and sweeping views of the valleys below. Grass covered the open space. Quinn imagined the presence of thousands of Inca citizens gathered in the plaza to participate in a town religious festival, or a speech from the emperor.

With these visions of ghosts from the past, Quinn turned into the stone city and navigated through a narrow alleyway.

As Quinn weaved his way through the city's maze of stone walls, he noticed how each stone fit together perfectly. No mortar held the stones in place, just detailed stonework. The walls were like puzzle pieces. Without reliance on mortar, the walls could bend and sway, withstanding earthquakes that shook the Andes. But never broke. Their form from the past echoed through the present.

As he turned the corner, Chris appeared.

"Quinn!" Chris shouted. "You startled me."

Tall stones surrounded Chris on both sides; echoes of the past manifested in the present.

"Where'd you go once we walked through the gate?" Quinn

asked.

"I knew there were some things from your life that you needed to work through," Chris said, "so, I decided to give you the space you needed to confront your past. Something I wish I would have done."

"What do you mean?" Quinn asked.

Chris smirked, masking a hint of sorrow.

"I wish I would have grappled with my parents and their ideas of success, their drive to buy more things," Chris said. "Ultimately, that's what killed us: the constant pursuit of more, even though more was never enough."

"I think I've finally reached that conclusion myself," Quinn said. "Before I came to Peru, I wanted it all: money, status, and things. Now, I've realized that success can't be measured by materials. Material success will never lead to happiness and fulfillment."

Chris looked through Quinn and saw a condor rise above the mountains. Quinn turned and watched the massive bird glide along the invisible currents.

"Beautiful," Quinn said, turning back toward Chris.

But Chris was gone. A thin fog filled the space where he used to stand. Something about Chris's message gave Quinn a second thought, something almost surreal.

Suppressing the idea, Quinn continued his walk through the ruins. Quinn came across a few alpacas grazing in the grass. The animals seemed unphased by Quinn's presence.

"Look at these beautiful animals," Francis said, appearing from somewhere in the city's alleyways.

"They're funny," Quinn said.

Francis smiled and slapped Quinn on the shoulder.

"The alpacas just move from one grass patch to another,

focused only on the moment," Francis said. "Look at how happy they are, simply content with being alive."

Quinn stood back and watched as the group of alpacas moved slowly, methodically.

"You're right," Quinn said. "Not thinking about where they came from. Not worried about where they're going to go."

"I wish we could all be like that," Francis said. "Look around at everyone here."

Quinn allowed his eyes to wander as he watched people funnel through the ruins.

"Here we are in Machu Picchu, surrounded by epic ruins, and we have people worrying about the next thing, the next train, where they're going to eat dinner, the best angle to take a picture to remember later."

"When they should simply be appreciating the moment," Quinn said. "That's where you really find happiness."

Francis smiled again. He nodded toward Quinn, and then returned to the alleyway from which he appeared. As Francis turned the corner, just out of Quinn's eyesight, Quinn dashed through the ruins to catch him. But, as Quinn turned the corner, Francis was gone.

That guy moves quickly, Quinn thought, slightly concerned.

Wandering aimlessly through an open field, Quinn took the path toward Huayna Picchu, the iconic mountain that overlooked Machu Picchu's famed stones. As he approached the mountain, he saw ancient stone stairs that led up the incline. The stones were cracked, yet sturdy.

Quinn propelled himself forward, taking the near-vertical path. After a few minutes, he turned to find Machu Picchu already far below him.

He noticed that Rosa was walking up the path. Quinn paused

to wait for her. When she reached Quinn, she stopped and smiled at him.

"Look at you, blazing an upward trail," Rosa said.

"Something told me that I had to explore this part of the city," Quinn said.

"Well then," Rosa said, "let's move forward together."

Rosa continued up the narrowing stairs. Quinn followed. His legs were fatigued from the trek and the morning's stairway, but he felt compelled to climb higher.

"Look at the beautiful jungle that surrounds us," Rosa said. "It's a shame that it has such a grim future."

Quinn slowed his pace and glanced at Rosa.

"How do you know things won't change for the better?" Quinn asked.

Rosa smirked.

"If humanity continues down its path of greed and consumerism," Rosa said, "places like Machu Picchu, the Amazon Rainforest, and the Andean climate will surely be destroyed."

"But what if we change our ways?" Quinn asked.

Quinn noticed a glimmer flash across Rosa's eye. She knew something, sensed something.

"Do you really think *humanity* can change their ways?" Rosa asked.

"It just starts with one person," Quinn said. "One person to change their habits. One person to change their priorities. One person to change the future."

Rosa paused midway along the stone staircase and looked back at Quinn.

"You've learned," Rosa said. "You've grown and changed. You're not the same person I met on the bus ride from Cusco."

"If I can change," Quinn said, "anyone can."

Quinn turned to look at Machu Picchu below him. The city was farther away than it was last time he looked. He could see the terraces that lined the mountainside beneath the city, showcasing the Inca's ingenuity in sustaining their land and their people. The city seemed so far out of reach.

"Just think," Quinn said, "someday, the future will look down on us and judge us for what we've done."

He turned toward Rosa for acknowledgment, but she was gone.

Confused, Quinn continued up the path. As the mountain grew steeper, the stones became more spread out. Stones stuck out from the mountainside; vast space fell beneath the path. Quinn jumped from one stone to the next, careful to maintain balance. One wrong step and he would fall to the valley below. Each weathered stone step seemed like it would disintegrate beneath his weight; each step brought him closer to death. Each step brought him closer to the ghosts of Machu Picchu.

Until he reached the top of the mountain. Another collection of buildings, jigsawed together by Incan builders, rested atop Huayna Picchu, overlooking the famed city below. A few small stone huts and viewpoints were packed onto the narrow mountain peak.

"Quinn," Antonio said.

Antonio stood on a stone platform overlooking Machu Picchu from high above the city. He waved his arms, motioning for Quinn to join him.

"This is one of my favorite spots in the entire city," Antonio said. "No one ever comes up here."

"That makes sense," Quinn said. "Those stairs were pretty treacherous."

Antonio laughed and leaned against an old stone wall.

"There are more sacred ruins on the peak directly across from us," Antonio said. "The Inca built that site in precise alignment with a sacred constellation. It acts as one star, and Machu Picchu acts as another. During *Inti Raymi*, the Winter Solstice, everything aligns perfectly. And today is that day: the day of perfect alignment."

Quinn nodded, unsure about why Antonio felt the need to bring this up.

"The Inca site across the valley from us is the burial site of many Incan emperors," Antonio continued. "You know, the Inca believed that the emperors were, in fact, gods. During *Inti Raymi*, the Inca used to honor their emperors, their gods, bringing the ancestors into the realm of the living."

Antonio watched Quinn's face for an expression of recognition, but he found a slow, perplexed nod instead. Antonio smiled and patted Quinn on the back.

"What did you think of your journey today?" Antonio asked.

"It was incredible," Quinn said. "Machu Picchu has a grasp on me. I can't quite explain it."

"That's the magic of the city," Antonio said. "The ghosts of Machu Picchu have a way of getting through to even the most skeptical travelers."

Quinn caught a glimpse of a condor soaring above the mountains. A sudden realization overcame him, stopping his breath.

"What do you mean *ghosts*?" Quinn asked.

Antonio smiled.

"Anything can happen on *Inti Raymi*, Mr. Thomas," Antonio said. "The space between the living and the dead is thinner than we think."

Quinn eyed Antonio curiously.

"It would seem that you learned a lot from your fellow

trekkers, Mr. Thomas," Antonio said. "Lessons that will truly change your life. If you let them, that is."

Antonio turned away from the Andean viewpoint, a perspective he had seen countless times. He walked away toward the descending path and disappeared from sight.

The Andes Mountains stretched out in front of Quinn in a panoramic view. Somewhere above the mountains, a condor flew away.

Chapter 20

The train station in Aguas Calientes was crowded with people returning to Cusco, their Machu Picchu trip completed. Orange lights sent sharp shadows across the otherwise dark platform. Travelers walked through illuminated spaces before shifting back into silhouettes. As Quinn looked around at the individual faces in the crowd, he could spot the people who had walked to Machu Picchu, masked with a thin layer of dirt and a well-used backpack. They stuck out compared to the day-trippers who still looked put together.

Quinn checked his pocket to ensure that his ticket remained secure. Then, he found an open space against a brick column and leaned against it. He was early for his train.

The hot jungle air had been overtaken by the chill that accompanied nighttime in the Andes Mountains. Quinn put his beanie over his ears and crossed his arms to ward off the briskness.

"Cold night," a man said, leaning against the column near Quinn.

"Sure is," Quinn said.

Something about his voice sounded eerily familiar.

A train arrived, tucking itself into the platform as its inner workings groaned. Steam rose from its engine, masking the crowd in a thin fog.

"That's my train," the man said.

The man moved quickly and merged into the crowd, disappearing into the haze. People funneled through the busy platform as they found their cars, but travelers with upcoming trains soon filled their spots in the crowd. Quinn took a drink from his water bottle, a reminder of the simple joys in his day.

As he stood on the platform, Quinn felt a sense of surreal accomplishment. Not the type of accomplishment that came with completing a dutiful task or a bucket list checkmark, but a sense of accomplishment that came with overcoming his own mind, completing a journey that he thought impossible.

He looked around at the crowd and wondered if anyone else held this same realization.

The whistle blew from a departing train, indicating that it was time for Quinn to board his passage back to Cusco. Less than a week had passed since he left the city, but so much had changed.

Absorbed into the moving crowd, he made his way into the correct train car. Built as a symbol of luxury from decades long ago, the train featured vibrant red carpet and golden fixtures, echoes of antiquated, colonial class distinction. Dark wood paneling lined the seats. Quinn removed his backpack and placed it in the compartment above his seat before he slid in against the window. The transparent glass felt cold as he leaned against it.

"Ticket, please," a man said.

He held out his hand and waited for Quinn to remove his ticket.

"Thank you," the man said.

He hole-punched Quinn's ticket and returned it to him.

"Enjoy the ride," the man said.

Quinn nodded and returned his attention to the window. He watched as passengers trickled into the train. Quinn leaned into the window and looked out into the platform. A reflective shimmer moved across the window.

He saw Chris standing on the platform, somehow illuminated among the crowd. His long hair, untied, flowed with the mountain breeze, connected to nature.

Francis emerged onto the platform, standing near Chris. Francis did not acknowledge Chris, and Chris did not acknowledge Francis. Yet, somehow, Quinn knew that they understood each other's presence.

From the other side of the crowd, Rosa appeared. Ducking her shoulder, she glided through tight spaces between travelers until she reached Chris and Francis. She stood near them, but did not make eye contact.

Quinn could not decide if the three trekkers were looking at him, or simply staring at the train. He thought they would be on the same train back to Cusco as he was, but they remained fixed on the platform, unwavering.

Then, a shadowed face moved through the crowd and stood near the trekkers. As the face lifted, the shadows dispersed. Charlie stood on the platform. He looked through the window at Quinn. Suddenly, Quinn felt a supernatural understanding. Charlie's penance had been served.

The final whistle bellowed from Quinn's train. As it slowly pulled away from the platform, Quinn looked out the window; his eyes fixated on Charlie, Chris, Francis, and Rosa. As he looked closer, he noticed them flicker. Pixelate. Transfigure between opaque and translucent.

The ghosts of Machu Picchu, Quinn thought.

Antonio's voice echoed through Quinn's mind.

His heart raced. He rubbed his eyes, refocusing on the three trekkers who stood out the window. Chris, Francis, and Rosa all moved their heads at once and waved at Quinn. Past, present, and future. They smiled with compassion, with the recognition that their lessons had been received.

And then, they dissipated, leaving the oblivious crowd shrouded in mystery, leaving Quinn to question his reality as his train sped into the darkness of the jungle.

Chapter 21

The van weaved through Cusco's narrow, cobblestone streets until it reached the hotel near Plaza de Armas. Quinn grabbed his backpack and jumped out. He thanked the driver and moved away from the vehicle. He stood on the sidewalk to get his bearings. The van screeched as it pulled away and disappeared around the corner and into darkness.

Quinn felt a void creep into his spirit. His sense of purpose for the last week had a singular focus: climb the mountain. Now, alone on a dark, cobblestone street, he had been released back into the wild, the wilderness of society, with no trail guide to point him the right direction.

It was up to him now.

Throwing his backpack over his shoulders, Quinn walked through the maze of Cusco's streets. The orange glow of street-lights reminded Quinn that he had returned to the familiarity of an urban environment.

Though it was dark, it wasn't late. The plaza buzzed with life. Families moved through major thoroughfares, from restaurants to shops. Teenagers gathered in the plaza to get away from their parents. The remnants of *Inti Raymi* remained present in the square.

Quinn found an empty bench near the center of the plaza. The golden statue of Tupac Amaru glared back at him, forcing him to confront his own family's role in colonial history, his own historical ghosts.

"*Buenas noches*," an old woman said as she walked by the bench.

She wore a tall, wide-brimmed hat and colorful clothing that draped around her, appearing to weigh her down. Her face held deep-set wrinkles, worn by time and sun, and creased by worry and laughter.

"*Buenas noches*," Quinn replied. "How's your night going?"

"Just fine," the woman said in Spanish.

As she smiled at Quinn, her eyes creased along the edges.

"Where are you from?" the woman asked.

Quinn smiled. His eyes drifted toward the mountains that rose above Cusco, sacred monoliths, illuminated by the full moon of the Winter Solstice.

"I'm from the United States," Quinn said.

The woman's face turned into something less jovial.

"Why do you say that with such sadness?" the woman asked.

"I'm not sure, really," Quinn said. "While I was here, I learned so much about myself and who I want to become. I don't know if I can bring that back to the States and actually follow through with it. What if I just fall back into my old routine? My old mindset?"

The woman smiled. The corners of her eyes crinkled with deep wrinkles, formed over decades of laughter and wisdom.

"Change is not easy, young man," the woman said. "Maybe it's up to you to bring that change home, back to your own people."

Again, Quinn looked at the statue of Tupac Amaru, the Inca

leader who battled against the Spanish invaders. The leader who rebelled against Spanish colonialism. The leader who fought for what he knew was right, who fought for change against impossible odds, who sacrificed everything for the greater good. The namesake for the American poet who called on his people to rise up and make the world a better place through change.

The woman nodded to Quinn and continued her slow stroll forward through the plaza. Some young people moved out of her way to make a clear path. A few kids exchanged kind smiles with the woman. Some adults did not notice the woman, but she adjusted her path before continuing toward her destination. Her feet navigated the old stones beneath her soles. Each step had its purpose. Each step, supported by builders from long ago, connected her to her city and guided her along her journey. Each step, its own ghost.

Quinn wondered what Charlie's path was like after the accident. He imagined Charlie being absorbed into the atmosphere, into the essence of life that seemed just out of reach for the living, an essence only palpable at altitudes found in places like the Andes Mountains, where the air was thin and the connection to Pachamama felt closer. He wondered how Charlie had done it. How Charlie had connected Quinn to the past, present, and future from somewhere behind the veil of life.

Quinn looked across the plaza to the well-lit cathedral, an imprint of Spanish colonialism. The stones fit together with the cityscape. He thought about what those stones used to support: Incan temples and houses. And before that, mountains and vegetation.

The city of Cusco had seen centuries of change and transformation, from one ruler to the next, from one ideology to another. Culture clashes and erasures. Cataclysmic forces, both natural and human. Yet, here it stood. A work in progress, yet still complete. Beautiful in its constant state of progression, withstanding the earthquakes, wars, and societal shifts that forced change upon it.

The thought of change lingered around Quinn, hanging like mist in his mind. Quinn leaned back against the bench and looked again at the statue of Tupac Amaru. It glowed gold, contrasted against the shadowed mountains. A force for change, burning in the Andes.

With a lightweight smile, Quinn lifted his eyes. He saw the moon shining high above him. Somewhere in the mountains, somewhere near Machu Picchu, a condor took flight.

Acknowledgments

First and foremost, I want to thank my family for giving me the inspiration and courage to be adventurous.

To my wife: thank you for always pushing me to be a better version of myself. Thank you for giving me unconditional love and support as I bounce ideas back and forth. Thank you for giving me time to be creative. I love you.

To my children: thank you for providing my life with so much light and life. Seeing the world through your eyes is a privilege and an honor.

To my parents: thank you for establishing an appreciation for cultures and places that I don't call home. Thank you for instilling the value of travel and experience, and for fostering a love for writing and storytelling.

To my teachers and mentors: thank you for cultivating my creativity and providing me with learning opportunities to hone the craft of the written word.

To my friends: thank you for adventuring with me. Thank you for always pushing me to expand my horizons and for diving into experiences that provide learning and growth.

And to my ancestors: thank you for paving the way forward. Thank you for your wisdom, your mistakes, and your successes that set the path for me to follow.

About the Author

Tom Malone was born and raised in Portland, Oregon, where he learned to love rain, coffee, and books. He spent time exploring the city, the forest, and the coast. Malone studied journalism and history at the University of Oregon, Spanish at *la Universidad de Oviedo*, and earned his master's degree from the University of Portland.

He has taken dozens of road trips throughout the United States and continues to travel throughout the world. Currently, Malone teaches secondary English near Denver, Colorado, where he camps, fishes, hikes, and snowboards often.

Also by Tom Malone

Captured

Michael had his entire future planned. He was going to propose to the love of his life and he had saved enough money to buy a house in the country. But, after a celebratory night out in the city, Michael wakes up in an underground tunnel system, the hidden network for the city's illicit activities. He's a prisoner, chained to a post. Captured. After a march through the underground tunnels, Michael is sold into servitude to a ship captain bound for Shanghai, destined for a life of misery, of invisibility, of disappearance. But, as Prohibition dawns in the United States, opportunities arise. Opportunities for gain, for loss, and for revenge.

Portlanders

Portland, Oregon: just another big American city. Tall buildings, millions of people, systemic problems, and a vibrant culture. In this collection of fictional short stories, take a walk through Portland from the perspectives of everyday people. Everybody experiences the city differently based on their own lenses, their own backgrounds, and their own motivations; it's the people who give a city its identity.

World History: A True Story

Explore the story of world history from its beginnings all the way to the modern day by looking at major civilizations, eras, people, and cultures that have shaped the world we live in. This brief overview of world history will spark interest, refresh learning, and provide a well-rounded look at how the world has reached its present state.

Across Americana

Ben's plan is unfolding perfectly. He is graduating from college. His dream job is set. Plus, his girlfriend is staying in his hometown and marriage is on the horizon. Then, on his college graduation day, he loses his job offer and his long-term girlfriend. Ben's best friend is leaving for the East Coast at sunrise. With nothing to hold Ben back, he embarks on a spontaneous cross-country road trip to New York City to begin an unforeseeable future. Along the journey, Ben encounters adventures that change his future forever.

Sloan Fitzpatrick: Middle School Journalist

Sloan Fitzpatrick is nervous about his first day of seventh grade. His best friend moved to another state. The school bully grew taller over the summer, while Sloan remained short. Plus, he registered for a Newspaper class just because his crush was the Editor-In-Chief, even though he knew nothing about journalism. After interviewing a city politician for his first assignment, Sloan finds himself wrapped up in the school newspaper. But he also finds himself caught in a political corruption investigation and he's in way over his head. Now, how's he supposed to handle seventh grade?

In the Shadow of the Spanish Sun

Jason embarks on a six-month journey to study abroad in Spain. When he arrives, he knows nothing but his own culture: an environment of greed, spiraling economic standards, and fast-paced rat races. After encounters with immigrant pick-up soccer, exotic cultures, and pushing the limit of fun, Jason dives too deep into these Spanish subcultures. He may find it difficult to return to his life in the United States. Then, he meets a girl. Will love turn him into an expatriate?

www.ingramcontent.com/pod-product-compliance
Lightning Source LLC
Chambersburg PA
CBHW030348180626
46812CB00007B/2807